YA
FIN

B+T

8-11 x

DOLTON PUBLIC LIBRARY DISTRICT

3 1146 00350 8474

STEPPING UP

D0107587

DOLTON PUBLIC LIBRARY DISTRICT
708 849-2305

For Susan, who
is always there for me,
always stepping up.

STEPPING UP

Mark Fink

WestSide Books ®
Lodi, New Jersey

Copyright © 2009 by Mark Fink
This book or parts thereof may not be reproduced in
any form, stored in a retrieval system or transmitted
in any form by any means—electronic, mechanical,
photocopy, recording or otherwise—
without prior written permission of the
publisher, except as provided by the
United States of America copyright law.

Published by WestSide Books
60 Industrial Road
Lodi, NJ 07644
973-458-0485
Fax: 973-458-5289

Library of Congress Control Number: 2008911814

International Standard Book Number: 978-1-934813-03-4
School Edition ISBN: 978-1-934813-19-5
Paperback ISBN: 978-1-934813-58-4
Interior design by Chinedum Chukwu

Printed in the United States of America
10 9 8 7 6 5 4 3 2 1

First Edition

STEPPING UP

1

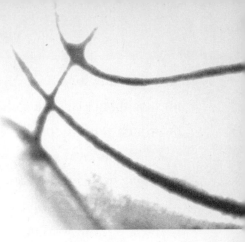

THE CURSE
OF AVERAGE

Did you ever have one of those days when your shoelace breaks, your hair sucks, your e-mail's down, you run out of matching socks, and the only one on the planet who really understands you is you? Well, I'm having one of those lives.

I'm fourteen years old, and the only thing I'm sure of right now is my name, Ernie Dolan. I guess you could call me pretty average. There's nothing wrong with average, but let's face it, after a while, average gets old. Show me one guy who wants to be just average. I'm 5'6", average for my age, but I have this fear that I've stopped growing forever. Guys are starting to shoot up past me, and I find myself looking up to more and more of them. Half the girls too, which really pisses me off.

I'm doing fine in school and I have a few friends, but I'm not exactly brimming with self-confidence. See, I have this little stutter, which cracks me up because there is no such thing as a little stutter. When you stutter, it's like the whole world stops. Ask any stutterer, and they'll tell you—of course, it's going to take them a while. You try surviving one day of school with a stutter—the stares, the jokes, the ridicule—and that's just from some of your friends. So, I'm working with a speech therapist twice a week, and I'm actually getting better. There are whole days when I'm stutter-free. But, when things get a little stressful, or in social interactions with strangers, my little friend appears, sabotaging my speech like a machine gun run amok.

I hardly ever stutter around Mike. That's Mike Rivers, my best friend in the world. Mike moved in across the street when we were six, and we've been best buds ever since. We ride to and from school together, study together, and eat at each other's houses five days a week. Mike grew three inches in the past year and is almost 5'10", way above average. He has dark brown hair, which is always in his eyes, and a small scar under his chin, thanks to a miscast fishing hook.

Mike and I know each other's deep dark secrets, including which girls we like. Mike's latest crush is on Karen Rogers, but he likes a new girl every week. Socially, I'm probably a year or two behind Mike; girls are just starting to appear on my radar. Tall girls.

Mike's one of those guys who's above average in a lot of ways: excellent student, great athlete, super comfortable around guys and girls. Even if he wasn't my best friend, I'd want to hang with Mike because, I like to think, he brings up my average. Cool as he is, Mike does have a couple of flaws, thank goodness. For instance, he's self-conscious about his ears, which he thinks are way too big.

The most important thing you have to know about Mike Rivers is that he's loyal. He's a great friend and is always there for me. He's always been patient with my stuttering, and in those moments when I get into a real jam, he'll bail me out of a sentence.

Another thing Mike and I share is our summer camp experiences. For the past four years, we've gone away together, and we alternate who chooses where. Last summer, I chose to go to Space Camp in Florida. This was by far the best camp yet. Mike and I got to go in a zero gravity simulator and float around like the astronauts. It was the weirdest, freest, most amazing experience ever. In fact, I still wear my "Gravity Sucks" T-shirt.

This summer, it was Mike's turn to pick, and he picked a basketball camp. I must confess, I'm a little worried. First of all, this is not your average basketball camp. Camp NothinButNet attracts a lot of good players, and the level of play is pretty intense. Mike and I'll play on our high school's freshman team—and we tried out for it just before school let out for the summer. We were on the team at our previous school, too. I was like, the eighth man, but Mike, was *the* man, leading us in scoring and rebounding. The game just comes easy to him. Mike is quick, with great hands and a soft shot. He's got lightning fast reflexes and an amazing instinct for always being where the ball is.

Me? I'm a pretty decent player—that is, I can shoot well, pass and dribble, and I know the game. But let's face it, no matter what the Declaration of Independence says, all men are *not* created equal. I'm not real fast, especially with the ball, not real tall, and I just don't possess that inner confidence that comes with great basketball instincts. Mike and I have played one-on-one in the driveway a thousand times. I've beaten him only once—when we were eight years old—and then only because he had a sprained shooting wrist.

So, you can see how this above-average basketball camp may not be the most comfortable place for an average kid like me. Then there's this other thing. It's the thing that's been creeping into my mind during geometry class and waking me in the middle of the night. For the past few months, things have been a little different between me and Mike. Let me try to explain: we're still best buds (I think), but Mike's kind of been moving in another direction. Being one of the jocks now, he's starting to hang with the cool people at school. Girls are now staring at him and coming up to him in the hallways—the same girls who look right through me. Mike has been steadily moving up the social food chain, while I'm still trying to crawl my way out of the swamp.

Mike calls me on my cell. "Dude, I need you. You've got to come over and help me pack."

No kidding. Mike may have a great crossover dribble, but he's not the most organized guy on the planet. We're leaving for camp in, like, fifteen hours, and he hasn't even started packing. I walk into Mike's room, and it looks like it was hit by a tornado. Underwear, shoes, shirts, and shorts are strewn everywhere, including a pair of boxers hung over a lamp shade. I have to navigate around two skateboards, a bike, and a PlayStation. As I walk, I feel the crunch of some kind of chips under my feet.

"What am I crunching on?"

"Fritos. Want some?"

"I'll pass."

"Boy, am I glad you're here," Mike says. "Got any suggestions?"

"Yeah. Call FEMA."

Mike laughs.

"Careful where you step," Mike says. "The cat's in here somewhere."

"Mike, you're hopeless."

"I know. That's why I have you. Now, where do I start?"

"Let's start with underwear and socks," I say.

"Oh, I get it. Underwear, socks—the first things you put on, the first things you pack. You're a genius, Ernie."

"No, you're just an idiot, Mike. Now, give me a hand here, will ya?"

Mike and I dive into a big pile of white clothes, and I show him how to fold them compactly. At one point, I pull out a purple bra. "Mike, is there something you want to tell me?"

"It's my sister's, doofus."

I take the next half hour and show Mike how to pack a suitcase (again). I stuff as many balled-up socks as I can into his Nikes, neatly fold his shirts and shorts, and demonstrate how to use every square inch of space.

"You're amazing, Ernie. Can you help me clean up my room?"

"Keep dreaming."

Mike gets on his laptop and goes to the camp website. Beautiful pictures come up as part of a virtual tour.

"Dude, look at that lake."

"Mike, you've showed me that ten times already."

"I heard the gym is like, brand new. This camp is going to be sweet."

"Yeah," I say, but not convincingly enough for Mike, who knows me all too well.

"What's with the look?"

"What look?"

"The look. It's the same look you had last week when you stepped in dog crap. Come on, E, you're not exactly pumped about this camp. What's up?"

"Okay. I'm a little worried."

"Worried about what?"

"It sounds pretty intense, Mike. Like they've got a lot of serious players."

"You're going to be fine. You know the game, and you're a great team player."

"Like that's not code for 'Get out of the way and give me the ball.'"

"I didn't mean it that way. You're better than you think, Ernie. And just think how much better you're going to be, going up against guys who can really play."

That's another thing I like about Mike. He's always positive and supportive.

"Chill, man, we're going to have a great time. We're rooming together, and hopefully, we'll play on the same team. It's you and me, the Two Musketeers. It's going to be an awesome two weeks."

"You're right." He puts his hand up, and I slap it. But I still can't shake this queasy feeling in the pit of my stomach.

2 NOTHINBUTNET

Monday, seven A.M. Mike's parents drop us off at a Greyhound bus station in downtown Chicago. The bus will make a few other stops to pick up passengers on what will be a four-hour ride to Camp NothinButNet. The camp is located on the shore of Lake Michigan near Grand Haven.

I try to blink the sleep from my eyes as we board the bus. It's not very crowded, so we have our choice of seats and head straight for the back. Mike likes to look out the window and I like the extra legroom in the aisle, so we make pretty good seatmates. Mike reaches into his backpack and takes out a small cardboard box. Smiling, he slowly opens it to reveal four glazed doughnuts.

"Breakfast. The most important meal of the day."

"Nice touch," I say, digging into a doughnut.

"Hey, it's the least I could do after you helped me pack."

"True," I say. "Did you ever find your cat?"

Mike shakes his head no. "But you know how he is—he loves to hide in piles of dirty laundry."

"Your laundry? Probably brain damaged from the fumes." Mike cracks up.

As the bus rumbles down the streets of Chicago, Mike and I settle in.

"When we get back, I think I'm going to ask out Debbie Sugarman," Mike announces.

"What happened to Karen Rogers?"

"Karen's nice, but I heard Debbie likes me."

"Oh. You heard if anybody likes me?"

"Not yet, but I'll let you know."

"Gee thanks," I say.

"Whatdya say we play some Madden?"

For the next hour, Mike and I play a very heated game of Madden NFL on Mike's portable PlayStation. My team beats Mike's easily in the first game, then I win the next game on a dramatic last-second pass play. Mike is pissed.

"Come on, best three out of five."

"Give it up, Mike. You lost twice. Deal with it." Mike pouts for a minute, staring out the window. He hates to lose at anything, which, of course, gives me even more pleasure when I beat him.

We both fall asleep for about an hour and wake up

when the bus pulls into another Greyhound station for a rest stop. We get off to use the restroom and buy some candy, then get back on the bus in our original seats. Some new passengers start to board, including two attractive teenage girls. Mike immediately sits up, at attention. "Ernie, chicks, twelve o'clock."

"Yes, I caught that."

"And did you also catch that they're hot? Let's go over and talk to them."

"I don't know. Now?"

"Yes, now. I swear the blonde was flirting with you."

"Why would she do that?" I asked.

"Because you're a stud. Come on."

I reluctantly get up from my seat and let Mike out first. I'm not at all good at this girl stuff, and those two doughnuts I scarfed down earlier are quickly making their way back up. I follow Mike as he leads me into the seats directly behind the girls.

"Hey, girls, welcome to my bus."

"*Your* bus?" the blonde asks.

"Yes, my name is Mike Greyhound. My family owns this bus company." Where does he come up with this stuff? Luckily, the girls somehow find this funny.

"Greyhound, huh? Wow. You'd think you'd have your own special luxury bus."

"Yeah, but I like to ride with the common people," Mike says. "Oh, this is my friend, Ernie."

"I'm Cameron, and this is Jennifer." Jennifer turns around in her seat, and now they're both facing us.

"Where you girls headed?" Mike asks.

"We're going to visit my cousin in Grand Haven," Jennifer says. "Where are you guys going?"

"We're going to a basketball camp. So, where do you go to school?"

"James Madison High in Oak Park. You?"

"We go to Central High in Evanston," Mike says with a straight face. "Going into eleventh grade." Unbelievable—he's just aged us two years.

"Us too," Cameron says.

"Doesn't he ever talk?" Jennifer indicates me, for some reason.

"Yeah, I t-t-talk." Uh-oh. Did I just stutter? Mike quickly jumps in.

"He talks fine. He just chooses his words carefully."

"That's right. I want to make sure they're accurate," I say, shooting a look at Mike.

So this goes on for over an hour, with Mike doing almost all the talking and me chiming in here and there, trying my best not to stutter or say something stupid. We pull into the Greyhound station in Grand Haven, Michigan, where the girls meet their cousin and we say our good-byes.

"I got their numbers and their MySpace sites," Mike announces proudly.

"I hope you also got a shovel."

"For what?"

"For all the bullshit you piled up on the bus. We're sixteen, in high school, and—I love this one—you're a part-time stunt man? It was all I could do not to bust out laughing, Mike."

"Ernie, they're older women. If they knew we were fourteen, they never would've talked to us."

"I gotta hand it to you, though. You are smooth around girls. How do you do that?"

"I have three sisters, remember?"

"Yeah," I say. "I just have a dog. It's not the same."

"They're just girls, Ernie. They're not from another planet."

"They are to me."

We take our luggage off the bus and catch a cab to the camp. After a few blocks of city streets, the cab turns off the main drag. Pretty soon, we're in a heavily wooded area, and between the trees, we can see the deep blue of Lake Michigan. The sun is shining on the water, illuminating a flock of birds dive-bombing over the surface. The road narrows and goes from asphalt to dirt, and minutes later, we pull into the front gate. A big sign reads:

WELCOME TO CAMP NOTHINBUTNET
YOU ARE ENTERING BASKETBALL HEAVEN

The first thing that strikes me as we get out of the cab is the sweet smell of really fresh air. The pine trees are huge, and the sky is a deep blue color you only see in pictures. It feels like we're a million miles from Chicago.

"This place is awesome," Mike announces. We pay the cab driver and carry our suitcases toward the main office.

"It's so quiet and peaceful out here," I say.

Just then, we hear the huge roar of an engine. A guy on a Harley-Davidson comes flying up the hill, kicking up clouds of dirt under his wheels. He skids to a stop in front of the main office, gets off the bike, and takes off his helmet. He appears to be in his late twenties and looks a little like Keanu Reeves in the *Matrix* movies.

"Hey, fellas, welcome to Camp NothinButNet."

"Do you work here?" I ask.

"You could say that. I coach some. I'm a counselor, lifeguard, dishwasher, gardener, and, oh yeah, I also own the place. Well, actually, my father owns the place. I just run it. I'm Tim Sanders."

Mike and I introduce ourselves and shake Tim's hand.

"Great to meet you guys. Why don't you drop your bags inside?"

Tim opens the door to the main office, which is a mix of rustic and hi-tech. The walls are made of logs and the wood floor creaks, but there are laptop computers and modern furniture all around. Basketball posters and photographs line the walls, most from the University of Michigan.

A very pretty woman walks in, carrying a first-aid kit. She has light sandy hair, big blue eyes, and a killer smile.

"New blood?" she asks.

"Yep. Laurie, meet Ernie Dolan and Mike Rivers," Tim says. "Laurie is our camp nurse."

"Welcome to camp, boys. Where are you from?"

"Chicago." We actually say it at the same time, like a couple of geeks.

"Oh. And do you always talk in unison?"

"No," we say, again together. Geek City. Laurie cracks up.

"I'm just messing with you. Make yourself at home, guys. I know you're going to like it here."

When she's out the door, I say to no one in particular, "She's hot."

"You think so?" Tim asks.

"Totally," I say.

"Yes, she is," Tim says. "And married. To me."

"You are so busted," Mike says, laughing. I just want to crawl into a hole.

I force a look at Tim. "I didn't mean . . . "

"Don't worry about it," Tim smiles. "But, Dolan, you better stay healthy and out of the nurse's office, because I've got my eye on you." He laughs, putting me at ease. I like this guy already. "Come on, fellas, let me show you around camp."

Tim escorts us around the grounds, starting with the road that leads to the lake. We cross a stream on a rickety rope bridge that swings back and forth with every step we take. We reach the shoreline and the camp dock, which moors about a dozen canoes and kayaks. The lake is huge and seems to stretch on forever.

"Our very own private lake," Tim says. "Of course, we share it with all of Michigan, Illinois, and Wisconsin."

Tim walks us along the lakefront to a fenced area that holds a big swimming pool and two Jacuzzis.

"This is our water sports center. You can't play B-ball twenty-four hours a day, so this is a great place to kick back and cool off. And those Jacuzzis are perfect for sore, aching muscles."

We head back toward the main building, where Tim shows us a typical cabin. It's rustic but very clean, with a wood floor, two bunk beds, a small closet, and a private bathroom and shower. It's got that musty cabin smell, but it's nicer than I expected it to be.

"Hey, nice digs," Mike says.

"Well, it ain't the Four Seasons, but it will be home for the next two weeks. You'll be sharing with two other boys."

We see the main dining hall and the game room, which has a big-screen TV, a couple of pool tables, air hockey, and ping-pong. Tim walks us over to the new gym and opens the door. It's awesome: a regulation full court with four other pull-down baskets for side games. There are several rows of bleachers on each sideline and stainless steel drinking fountains in the four corners. I'm really impressed by the lighting. It's the best-lit gym I've ever been in. For anyone who's ever played on outside courts with bent rims and in dark, dingy gyms that were 120 degrees, this place is heaven.

"It's amazing," I say.

"Isn't it? We modeled it after the University of Michigan gym. That's my alma mater."

"You played there?" Mike asks.

"Well, I mostly rode the bench there. But I got in a few games."

"Can we shoot around?" Mike asks.

"Not yet, guys. No one's allowed in the gym unsupervised. Don't worry, you'll be spending enough time in here. Why don't you two look around, meet some of the guys, and we'll get together a little later, when all the campers have arrived."

Mike and I walk around the grounds for a while, admiring the serene setting.

"Didn't I tell you this place was cool?" Mike says.

"Yes, you did, and yes, it is."

We come to an outdoor court on a blacktop, where four kids are shooting around.

"Let's go play," Mike says.

"You go ahead." I really don't want to play right now. Then, from the court, one of the boys waves to us. He's tall with dark hair and looks like the ultimate jock.

"Hey, guys! You want to play threes?"

Mike looks at me, and I look straight back at him. "Come on, Ernie, it's just a little pick-up game. You'll be on my team. No pressure." No pressure. Sure, not for him.

"You guys down or not?" Mr. Jock was getting impatient.

"Yeah." Mike answers for me.

"Thanks a lot, man. I said I didn't want to play."

"Relax, E, it'll be fun." Mike's already on his way down there, and now I have to play.

There are times in your life when you get that feeling in your gut about something, when you just know deep inside you shouldn't do something. This is one of those times. But do I listen to my gut? No, I go ahead and play. Big mistake.

3
FIRST IMPRESSIONS

I follow Mike down to the court, and my legs are getting heavier every second. We introduce ourselves and meet our first group of fellow campers. There's Allan, Jamal, Jack, and the jock who's been doing all the talking. His name is Rick Craig. He's even taller up close, with broad shoulders, thick calves, and large hands—just the right tools for basketball. He looks to be at least a year older than us, but you never know. There's something about this guy I don't like. There's no legitimate reason to feel this way, but once again, in my gut, there is a certain vibe I'm picking up. Maybe it's the way his upper lip curls down into a permanent smirk.

We break into two teams of three. Mike actually makes the teams, grabbing me, then Allan by the arm and pulling us off to one side.

"Whatever," Rick says. "We'll go to eleven by ones.

I'll shoot for outs." He takes the ball to the top of the key and arcs up a feathery shot that touches nothing but net, and I'm not sure it even touched that. Mike, who never backs away from a challenge, lines up to guard Rick. I immediately size up Jack and Jamal and decide to guard Jack, who is thirty pounds overweight and, hopefully, slow.

I know it's just a stupid, meaningless pick-up game, but I'm still way too nervous and I don't know why. My legs are like lead, my stomach's like the inside of a blender, and my mouth is so dry it should be designated a fire hazard.

Rick flips the ball in to Jamal, who gives it back to Rick. Rick moves with ease, dribbling the ball beautifully with either hand, his eyes never looking down. With Mike covering him pretty well, Rick shoots. Well, I think he shoots and Mike sure thinks he shoots, but Rick deftly fakes the jumper, gets Mike in the air, then waltzes in for an easy layup.

Mike is pretty embarrassed, which doesn't happen often on the court. Rick can't hide an even bigger smirk. "That's one." It's the way he says it. There's a cockiness that coats his voice, a cockiness I've never heard before. He may as well have said, "That's one of hundreds you're going to see, and you guys have no business being on the same court with me."

On the next possession, Rick passes to Jamal, who misses a jump shot. Mike gets the rebound and faces Rick offensively for the first time. With payback surely on his mind, Mike crosses Rick over and drives in for a nice left-handed layup. Rick offers his props: "Nice move. Very smooth."

Getting the ball again, Allan inbounds it to Mike. Mike snaps me a bounce pass, then sets a screen on my man, Jack. I take the advantage and dribble toward the basket. Jack slips and goes down, giving me a clear path to the hole. I can already feel the sweat running down my face. I take off on my left foot for the layup, but somehow jam the ball against the rim, missing it badly.

"Choke," Rick announces, grabbing the rebound. This hurts as much as the blown shot, but any way you look at it, I *did* choke. I've made that shot thousands of times. Now, anyone who's ever played this game knows that making your first shot is the ultimate confidence builder. Conversely, missing your first shot, especially the ugly way I missed mine, works on your head in the opposite way. If I was nervous before, now I'm really tense. I can actually feel my muscles tighten up, and I'm having trouble getting a breath. To make matters worse, a little crowd of campers has gathered around the court and are watching my every move.

I turn to Mike. "My ba-ba-ba-bad." There it is. My stutter is back. Mike gives me a sympathetic look and motions with his hand for me to calm down, all the while playing defense on Rick. My mind already isn't into this game, and now all I can think about is my stutter, wondering how long it's going to stay and how bad it's going to be.

Rick scores two more baskets, and Mike matches him. Mike is elevating his game to approach Rick's level, and the two of them are quickly developing a healthy respect for each other.

"That's a nice shot, Smooth," Rick says after Mike hits another fadeaway jumper. We're down 8-7 when Mike makes a great steal and hits me with a quick pass. I see it coming, but it goes right through my hands out of bounds.

"Ernie!" Mike cries out in frustration. He calls time out and takes me off to the side. "What's up with you, man?"

"I don't know, I just ca-ca-ca-can't . . . "

Rick comes over and hears this. "Ca-ca-ca-can't what, Choke, can't catch? Or ca-ca-ca-can't talk?" This brings instant laughter from everyone except Mike, who knows how uncomfortable this is for me. Mike makes a quick motion for Rick to back off, then smacks me on the back and gives me one of his "it's going to be okay" nods.

Thirty seconds later, I'm wide open at the free-throw line and Allan hits me with a pass. I hoist up an awful-looking air ball that falls two feet short. It's like I'm trying to shoot a bowling ball.

"That was ugly, Choke," Rick says, laughing. Mike glares at him, but doesn't say anything. Now totally psyched out, I just want to get this damn game over with. I manage to go through the motions and don't take another shot. Allan and Mike keep it close, but we lose 11-8. Rick hits nine of the eleven shots. Mike makes seven out of our eight. Rick goes up to Mike and slaps his hand.

"You've got some game, Smooth."

"Yeah, you too," Mike says. Rick doesn't even look at me. Mike and I walk off the court. There's not a whole lot I can say to him.

"Sorry, Mike. Could I play any w-w-w-worse?"

"Calm down, Ernie. Forget it.

"Yeah, but I l-l-let you down."

"You didn't let anybody down, E. It's just a stupid pick-up game."

"Right." But I know it's a whole lot more than just a stupid pick-up game. It was a first impression, and first impressions are huge. To everyone who saw me today, I'm a guy who totally sucks at basketball. That wasn't the real me out there, but they don't know that. They saw what they saw, and it's all about perception. First impressions define and label you, sometimes for life. Rick Craig is already giving out nicknames. Mike is "Smooth." And I'm "Choke."

I'm starting to think that this could be a very long couple of weeks.

4 THE ROOMIES

Mike and I walk over toward the main camp office, and my mind races. What exactly just happened to me? I'm not sure, but I chalk it up to nerves. I was really nervous, and it got inside my head. I put all this pressure on myself, and the more I tried, the worse I played. As my anxiety increased, my stuttering came back, causing even more anxiety.

Mike looks at me and sees I'm somewhere else. "You okay, E?" I nod. "It was one lousy game. Just forget it." He's right. I just wish it was that easy.

We pick up our room assignment and carry our bags up a winding hill to cabin 24. Walking into the cabin, we come face to face with a tall African American kid wearing a Minnesota Timberwolves jersey.

"Hey, guys. I'm Derek Singleton."

"I'm Mike. This is Ernie. You from Minnesota?" Mike asks.

"Yeah, St. Paul."

We shake hands. "What's St. Paul like?" I ask.

"Cold. Where you guys from?"

"We live right outside Chicago."

"Your Bulls are getting good again," Derek says.

"Yeah, but try getting tickets now," I say.

As Derek unpacks, he takes out a Camp NothinBut-Net T-shirt.

"You got a T-shirt already?" Mike asks.

"I went here last year."

"What's it like?" Mike asks.

"Tight. You like hoops, this is the place. I got dibs on a bottom bunk, okay?"

"Go for it," Mike says.

So, Derek starts setting up his things, taking the bottom bunk of the bed on the left. I also prefer a bottom bunk and Mike's cool with the top, so we set ourselves up at the other bed. Derek doesn't say much, but we draw him out and learn that he's fifteen and goes to a small private school.

A few minutes later, a porky, goofy-looking kid with bright red hair lumbers into the cabin. He's carrying a duffle bag, a bright red pillow, a case of CDs, and a giant bag of barbecue potato chips, several of which are in his mouth.

"Don't get up," he says, which prompts all of us to scramble to our feet and take things from his hands. "Thanks, roomies. I'm Albert Mann."

There is something about this kid that just makes you want to laugh. It could be the red hair, or the goofy grin, or those eyes, which dart around the room, sizing everything up. "Think you guys can help me bring in the rest of my stuff?"

"There's more?" Derek asks.

"Just a few odds and ends," Albert says.

Outside on the cabin porch is another duffle bag, a boom box, three bags of food, an air purifier, and a small microwave oven. Derek, Mike, and I all look at each other, then over at Albert.

"You brought a microwave oven? Is that allowed?" Mike asks.

"Of course not. But now we have a kitchen that's open twenty-four seven. What do you guys want for lunch? I have lasagna, beef burritos, or shrimp fettuccini." Derek, Mike, and I crack up and help Albert in with his haul. We pile up his stuff in the middle of the cabin, and it takes up half the room.

"Dude, it's like you're going away for a year," Derek says.

Albert says, "I know. All this stuff and only one pair

of underwear. Dibs on a bottom bunk." Derek looks at him and points to his stuff already there.

"Uh, sorry, you were the last guy in."

"Okay, no problem. I just gotta warn you, I wet the bed." The look on Derek's face is priceless. He actually starts to move his stuff off the bed. "Kidding." Mike and I laugh, and a relieved Derek cracks a little smile.

Albert tells us he's from Wisconsin and the oldest of eight children. Says he loves hot dogs and once ate thirty-three in fifteen minutes to win a contest. Claims his father is a TV weatherman. Frankly, I don't know what to believe, but the guy is very entertaining.

"Anybody want to go down and check out the lake?" Mike asks.

"Sure, I'll go," Derek says.

I want to finish unpacking, so I hang back with Albert. Albert waits until they leave, then comes up to me.

"Don't worry about it."

"Worry about what?"

"The way you played."

"You saw?"

"Yeah. And I know that's not how you play. I could see how nervous you were."

"Thanks." I like this guy already. "Yeah, I really melted down out there."

3508474

Dolton Public Library District

35

"I can already tell you're better than me. Basketball isn't exactly my game."

"Really? Then why come to a basketball camp?"

"Let's see," Albert says. "Last year, my parents sent me to a fat camp, and I gained eight pounds. So this summer, I thought I'd try this. I'm just here to run around and have as much fun as possible."

Albert seems like a guy who can have fun anywhere. And he's already made me feel a whole lot better about things. I really like this guy.

"So, your friend, Mike, can he take a joke?"

"Yeah, he's cool. Why?"

"Meet Sly." Albert reaches into one of his duffels and pulls out a big hairy rat and throws it to me. I jump three feet back, and it falls at my feet with a thud. "Looks pretty real, huh?"

"Very real," I say, picking up the hairy, slimy rat by the tail and looking into its tiny beady eyes. It's heavier than it looks.

"Got any suggestions where to put him?" Albert asks.

"I know exactly where to put him," I say.

I open the zipper of Mike's suitcase and stick the rat under some underwear, then zip it back up.

"Sweet," Albert says, with that silly grin.

A while later, Mike and Derek return and finish unpacking.

"I left you the bottom two drawers," I say, pointing to the dresser near our bunk. Mike unzips his suitcase and marvels at the neatness.

"This is a work of art, Ernie. Maybe I shouldn't even unpack it."

"No," I say, "you really should unpack."

When Mike picks up a pile of underwear and carries it to the drawer, the rat drops out. Mike screams and runs into the bathroom. Derek is also startled and jumps back three feet. Albert and I double over with laughter as Mike cautiously sticks his head out of the bathroom door.

"Gotcha," Albert says, picking up the rat and showing that's it's a fake.

"That is *so* not funny," Mike says, embarrassed.

"That is so *totally* funny," I shoot back. Albert gives the rat to Mike, who holds it up by the tail like it's going to bite him.

"It looks so alive," Mike says.

"It was once," Albert informs him. Mike drops the rat.

Just then, we hear some chimes from a speaker in the ceiling. "Welcome to Camp NothinButNet. Our first all-camp meeting will be in the gym in five minutes. See you all there."

⊕

We all walk down to the gym and take a seat in the bleachers. After everyone files in, there are about seventy-five boys, most sitting with their cabin mates, like the four of us. Some boys know each other from previous camps and call out to their friends. A lot of guys seem to know Rick Craig, who attracts a crowd.

Tim Sanders jogs onto the court and faces the assembly. His voice is amplified by a clip-on microphone attached to his shirt. "Hi, and welcome to Camp NothinButNet. Now, this is a basketball camp, but it's much more than just that. When you leave here, I guarantee that each one of you will be a better basketball player. And hopefully, you'll be a better person as well. We stress fundamentals, sportsmanship, discipline, and personal responsibility. You're not only going to learn the right way to set a pick, you'll also learn how to be a teammate and a friend."

Tim then introduces his wife, Laurie, and Mike turns to me. "Any more comments, champ?" I shake my head and zip my mouth closed.

"I'm Laurie, and I'm the closest thing you're going to have to a mother for the next two weeks. I'm also a registered nurse, so if you're not feeling well or you're injured, I'm the one you want to see." Laurie goes on to tell us about the standard safety precautions, mentioning sunburn, poison ivy, mosquitoes, dehydration, and water safety.

Tim then briefly explains the program. We'll have several days of drills, going from station to station, each emphasizing a different aspect of the game. All the while, the coaches will be evaluating us. Then the coaches will assemble eight teams, balancing them to be as equal as possible. The eight teams will play a series of games, with four teams making the playoffs. Then those four will play off to determine the camp championship. It's about more than just prestige; every member of the winning team wins a free session of camp for next summer. The final night of camp will be highlighted by an awards banquet.

"One more thing," Tim says. "No laptops or video games are allowed at camp. Cell phones can be used only after eight P.M. You're in beautiful surroundings in a great program. It won't kill you kids to be less wired up for a couple of weeks. That's it. Let's eat."

The dining hall is pretty much a regular cafeteria, only the food smells better. Several rows of tables fill most of the room, and there's a long buffet line where we take a tray and choose our food. Tonight, they're serving three main dishes: chicken, meat loaf, and trout—something for everyone. Mike and I fill our trays with several selections and a few desserts, then meet Derek and Albert at a table with some other campers.

Most campers seem to be eating with their cabin mates, but social lines are already being drawn. There is one table that is the center of attention, the hot table. Holding court at this table is Rick Craig, who has the other kids hanging on his every word. They are talking animatedly and laughing freely, unlike the rest of the room, where everyone is just feeling each other out. Just looking at this table makes me feel uneasy. It doesn't help that the meat loaf is prepared with some kind of spice that was put in just to destroy my stomach.

"Is this meat loaf the best, or what?" Albert says, stuffing his face with another shovelful. I get the feeling this kid would eat a basketball if he could fit it into his mouth, and who knows? He probably could.

After dinner, we all file into the gym for a camp first-night tradition: the best basketball movie ever, *Hoosiers*. It's about a small-town Indiana high school team that defies the odds to win the state championship over schools ten times the size of theirs. It's totally real—a true story, in fact—and it has some of the coolest basketball scenes you'll ever see in a movie.

At the end of the movie, when the team wins the state championship in an amazing game, the campers let out a huge roar. If ever something were going to get you pumped up to play basketball, this would be it. Even *I'm* ready to lace 'em up.

5

INTO THE GYM

The gym is primed and ready. All the baskets are in place, and a rack of basketballs stands under each one. We campers are in the bleachers at nine A.M. sharp, all wearing our camp practice uniforms: black shorts and gray T-shirts emblazoned with the Camp NothinButNet logo.

Tim Sanders sprints into the gym, wearing the same uniform and looking like he can still play.

Tim shouts, "Are you guys ready for some basketball?"

The roar from us campers says it all.

"Good, that's what we're all here for," Tim says. "I'd like to introduce my coaching staff, so pay attention. One of these guys is going to be your coach." The coaches are mostly current and former college players, with a few former NBA guys thrown in. Rumor has it that Magic Johnson, who played college ball at Michigan State, pops in for a surprise appearance for some sessions.

Tim explains that the next three days will be nothing
but drills: everything from the fundamentals to the more
intricate parts of the game. We'll break into groups and go
to one of six stations. Each station emphasizes a different
skill or aspect of the game, and we will rotate through
every station.

Mike and I file out of the bleachers and end up in the
same group, which is comforting. Our first station covers
the passing game. Ed Dexter, a junior guard at Notre
Dame, greets us with a warm smile.

"Hey, fellas. Welcome to Passing 101. I'm going to
show you the art of passing and how good passing can
change a game. You're going to see how a well-timed,
well-delivered pass can be every bit as exciting as making
a basket. There will be no shooting at this station. Anyone who takes a shot at the basket is gonna sit his butt
down for the rest of the morning."

I'm not a big scorer, so I've always concentrated on
being a pretty decent passer, trying to feed my teammates
whenever I can. But I soon find out that there is so much
more to passing than I ever realized.

Ed breaks the twelve of us into pairs and demonstrates
the proper way to throw the chest pass. He emphasizes
footwork and follow-through, which helps us snap crisp,
accurate passes. We work on the bounce pass, which is

preferred by most coaches because it's less likely to be stolen. Ed shows us when to use the bounce pass and when not to, and how to direct the pass to the exact spot we're aiming for. He goes down the line, giving pointers and encouragement.

We work on one-hand passes and behind-the-back passes, which, according to Ed, have their place—not to be fancy, but to deliver the ball when an opponent is least expecting it. Then we work on outlet passes, the kind made when a player grabs a rebound and wants to start a fast break.

After an hour of passing drills, we rotate to the shooting station, where Serge Petrovich greets us. Serge is from Russia and plays ball in Europe. He's 6'10" and has a buzz cut, a goatee, and twinkling eyes. Standing next to Serge, I get a sense, for the first time, of just how big real basketball players are. Looking up at him to make eye contact is like looking up at the stars.

Serge speaks broken English in a squeaky Russian accent. "Shooting eez all foon-da-mentals. Once you get dem down, eet's all in-stink." We all laugh at his English, and Serge shrugs. "Okay, I know I talk funny, but to me, all of you talk funnier. Remember, I shoot better than I talk, so give me your ears." Serge demonstrates the art of shooting, and suddenly, no one's laughing. Serge goes all around the court, hitting shots from every distance and angle—over twenty in a row. It's a beautiful thing to watch, and we're all blown away.

"Remember, guys, elbow een, extend dee arm, use your legs, release off fingertips, and follow true."

I've never heard shooting broken down this way, and I've never quite heard the English language broken down this way either, but I must say, the guy knows what he's talking about. Serge rolls out some balls, and we try it. After a few misses, I try to follow Serge's method and sink five shots in a row. He sees the last one go in and gives me a quick wink.

Next, Serge covers shooting layups with both the right hand and the left, reminding us to take off on the opposite foot. I'm feeling good and starting to relax. A loose ball rolls over to another court, and when I chase it down, I come face to face with Rick Craig. "How's it goin', Choke? Hit the rim yet?"

"Nope, just all net," I say, then run back to my group. I'm proud of my response, but I know this guy's going to be trouble.

The morning session goes by in a flash, and we break for a barbecue lunch down by the lake. Mike and I get our hot dogs and sit at a table.

"So, Ernie, didn't I tell you this camp was going to be great?"

"You did. And it is. These coaches really know what they're doing."

"We just got started and I already feel like I'm getting better," Mike says. Coach Petrovich takes a seat at our table.

"Thanks for the shooting lesson, Coach, it really helped," I tell him.

"You're welcomed. Who are you again?"

"I'm Ernie Dolan. This is my friend, Mike Rivers."

"Good to meet me," Coach says, and I find myself trying to hold back a laugh.

"So, what's it like playing professionally in Europe?" Mike asks.

"Good, but long way from NBA. I make some money, play couple years, but den haf to get real job. Can't play basketball forever." Serge looks sadly out at the lake.

"You can always coach," I say.

"Yes, but must learn gooder English first."

"I'd trade you my English for one good dunk," I say.

"Deal," Serge says. "But you gonna need ladder."

We return to the gym and the remaining stations: dribbling, rebounding, offense, and defense. The coaches watch carefully, scribbling on their clipboards as they evaluate each of us. By the end of the afternoon, we're all tired, but it's time to face the dreaded wind sprints. Each camper is timed in a sprint up and down the length of the court. Being fairly fast, I do pretty well, beating Mike and a bunch of other guys and logging the fifteenth-best time. The fastest time goes to Rick Craig, who looks like he expected nothing less.

Basketball ends at four, and we're on our own until dinner at six-thirty. Derek sacks out for a nap, and Mike, Albert, and I decide to hang out at the pool. A few kids are already in the pool, while others lie on towels on the deck. We stake out a space, and the sun feels great on my tired muscles.

"I'm beat," Albert says. "I never got this tired at computer camp."

"It's good for you, man, it'll get us all in great shape," Mike says.

I close my eyes and start to soak in the sun, feeling relaxed for the first time since I've been here. Then, I hear that voice.

"Who's down for pool volleyball?"

It's Rick Craig, arriving with his entourage. Within seconds, all eyes and ears are turned to him. Rick quickly organizes a pool volleyball game, and he and Jamal pick the teams. Rick picks Mike first, and Mike springs to his feet like an eager puppy. This really pisses me off. I know Mike doesn't love the water; in fact, he's a little afraid of it. But there's something about Rick Craig that seems to draw people in. It's like he's this big, powerful magnet, and everyone else is a bunch of paper clips. Rick and Jamal each pick three guys, which leaves out exactly two of us—me and Albert.

"Sorry, Dolan, but no chokes allowed," Rick says.

"Like I want to play anyway," I shoot back.

The volleyball game is in the shallow end of the pool, but I can tell Mike's still uncomfortable. He never dives for a ball (which is the fun part) and rarely sinks in below his shoulders. Still, he fakes it well enough to hit a few good shots and blend in with Rick and his friends.

Albert turns to me and says, "You really do want to play, don't you?"

"Yes, no . . . I don't know."

"Forget it. You don't need these guys, Ernie. Screw 'em. Craig's a major asshole."

"You got that right."

"The way I see it," Albert says, "is that the world is full of guys like Craig. There's always going to be guys like that ragging on guys like us."

I wasn't sure if I liked where this was going. "What exactly do you mean, 'guys like us'?"

"You know, we're not jocks, we're not exactly cool, we don't attract attention . . . but it's guys like us who eventually run the world . . . people like Bill Gates and those Google guys."

"Thanks, Albert, but I'm not some computer geek, so don't lump me in with you guys."

"Okay, but you're totally missing my point, dude. There's an advantage to being a little geeky, or a little less cool. It lets us fly under the radar. People underestimate us. Then, when we do something special, BOOM, we shock the world."

"Where do you come up with this stuff?"

"Hey, I've been out of the loop my whole life. It gives you a lot of time to think. Guys like Craig, they're gonna get theirs."

"Not soon enough," I say.

"How 'bout right now?" Albert pulls his fake rat out of a paper bag.

"Sweet."

"Let's see if Mr. Jock can spike this."

This is going to be good. Tense, but good. I watch with great interest as Albert carries the rat in his towel and casually wanders by the shallow end of the pool. At the perfect moment, he drops the rat into the water, two feet from our friend Rick. It's only a matter of seconds before Rick turns to hit the ball and sees Sly. He screams like a girl and instantly catapults himself out of the water. Albert and I crack up as Mike picks up the rat and shows Rick that it's fake. Rick's not laughing, and neither is Mike.

"You think that's funny, losers?"

"Funny enough," Albert says.

"It's totally lame," Mike says, taking Rick's side.

It's getting less funny as Rick advances toward us. He picks up the rat and rifles it right at Albert's head. Albert ducks, and the rat hits the outdoor clock, shattering its plastic cover. Now all the kids are laughing except Rick, whose face is getting redder by the minute. He steps closer to Albert, but just then, two of the coaches enter the pool area.

"I'm going to get you for this, Mann." Rick promises.

"Me and my rat are shaking," Albert says.

Rick Craig is clearly embarrassed. Something tells me this kid doesn't get embarrassed too often. I make a mental note to buy myself a fake rat.

⊕

We're in line at the dining hall, and I'm starved. I follow Mike through the line, loading my plate up with roast beef, mashed potatoes, vegetables, and three desserts. As we head for the table where our roommates sit, I hear Rick Craig's voice over the noise.

"Yo, Smooth, over here."

Rick is motioning Mike over to a vacant seat he's saved at his "A" table. This should be interesting. I continue to my "D" table and put my tray down. Mike hesitates for a second like a deer caught in the headlights. He then veers toward Rick's table and, right before he sits down, looks over at me with an apologetic shrug. I shrug back as sarcastically as I can. Two days into camp, and my best friend has switched tables. Talk about a rat.

I sit there eating my lumpy mashed potatoes, and I can't help thinking about what Albert said earlier at the pool. Life is just not fair if an idiot like Craig can be so popular. I wonder what it's like to be the guy everyone respects and wants to hang with. Just once, I'd like to be that guy.

6 THE LUCK OF THE DRAW

It's day three, and the heat has snuck up on us, sucking out all the breathable air for miles. I'm awakened by a mosquito trying to eat through my forehead. I slap it away, and it falls into an open bag of potato chips on the floor. Albert walks by, picks up the chips, and starts to dig in.

"You don't want to eat those."

"Oh, but I *do*, Dolan. Look, if you want a couple, I'll share."

"You have no idea what's in there."

Albert reads the label. "Let's see: lime, vinegar, salsa flavor, sea salt . . . "

"And much, much more," I say. After all, what's one more mosquito in Albert's stomach?

After a shower, I head down to the cafeteria for breakfast. It's D-day, Draft Day, the day the coaches announce the teams. Everyone's a little anxious, as we'll be stuck on these teams for the rest of camp. I'm more than a little anxious, and I'm not sure I can even hold down my breakfast.

I take a shortcut, darting between two cabins. Some idiot is carrying a stack of boxes that towers over his head, blocking his view. He bumps into me, and a trophy falls out of the top box, heading for the concrete. I dive for it, grabbing it like a wide receiver, just before it hits the ground. I look up and see Tim Sanders, peeking at me from behind a box.

"Great catch. You play football too?"

"Afraid not."

"Well, with those hands, maybe you should. Thanks for the save, Dolan."

"You're welcome, Mr. Sanders."

"Call me Tim. Heck, you've already hit on my wife."

"Which, I guess, I'll never live down."

"Probably not. But you've just redeemed yourself by saving me forty bucks."

"Cool trophy," I say.

"Yeah, and that's just the second-place trophy. Want to see something really cool?"

Tim motions for me to follow him, handing me a few of the boxes to carry. He leads me to the main building and into his office.

"Don't tell anyone you've seen this. Promise?"

"Promise."

Tim takes his keys and opens a tall cabinet. He carefully takes out an awesome-looking three-foot-high gold trophy. There is a figure of a player following through on a jump shot, and a bright gold ball already in the net.

"That is, like, the most amazing trophy I've ever seen."

"I know. I designed it myself. This is what you'll be playing for, Dolan. Only the very best can claim to be camp champions. So, how do you like it here so far?"

"Fine, I guess."

"Fine, you guess? That's how you describe a trip to the dentist."

"Okay, I guess I'm still just getting used to things, that's all. There're some really good players here, and I'm just hoping to keep up."

"I hear you. Just get the lay of the land, then settle in and play your game. You'll be fine. And listen, if you ever need anything, ever have a question or a problem, come see me, okay? I owe you one."

"No you don't, Tim."

"Yeah, I do. The stupid trophy shop takes three weeks to make a trophy. That was a big-time catch."

"Okay, since you owe me one, do you know what team I'm on and who my coach is?"

"Yes, I do."

"And that would be?"

"That would be spoiling all the anticipation of Draft Day. You'll find out in a few minutes."

"Fine," I say. "But you still owe me one." Tim smiles, and I head to the gym.

⊕

The gym is buzzing with excitement. Tim calls for the coaches to join him, and each will call off the names of the campers on his team. I'd love to play on the same team as Mike, but I know the odds are against it.

Albert Mann's name is called for the first team, the Hawks, and he climbs out of the bleachers and takes a goofy bow. "I'm here to announce that I'll be skipping camp basketball to go directly into the NBA." The campers hoot and laugh, and some toss headbands and sweat socks at Albert. He loves every minute of it, and I love his carefree spirit.

Mike ends up on the Pacers, along with our roommate Derek. I listen for my name and hope to join him, but it's not in the cards.

The fifth team is the Kings, coached by Serge Petrovich, the funny Russian guy who murders the English language.

"Eeer-nee Dolan." I'm the first one called onto Serge's team. This is good. I like this guy, and I know he'll be a terrific coach. Serge greets me with a high five when I reach the floor.

"Goood to have yourself, Eeer-nee."

"Myself is good to be had," I say, trying to learn his language.

A few other guys get called, and then Serge calls out the one name I was dreading to hear. "Reek Craig." Craig bounds down from the bleachers and struts over to our team, as if he's waiting for us to break out into applause. My ninety seconds of happiness comes to a screeching halt as my heart instantly sinks down to my sweat socks. Rick slaps hands with his new teammates, even me. I think, *okay, now that he's a teammate, maybe he'll change, maybe he'll warm up to me.* Then, Rick leans over to my ear and whispers, "Don't blow it for us, Choke." So much for warming up.

How did this happen? The odds against Rick being on my team were something like 7-1. I want to say something to someone, demand a trade. Better not. I'm not a whiner, and I don't want to be branded as one. I'll just try to make the best of it.

We practice as a team for a few hours, and later in the

day, we play our first game. I don't start, but I know my time's coming, and my stomach knots up accordingly.

We're playing the Spurs, who have a couple of pretty good guys, but no great athletes. Rick Craig, playing a guard/forward position, dominates, hitting twenty-footers and slashing to the basket for easy layups. The guy can play, I'll give him that. By the end of the first quarter, we're up by eleven points.

Coach Petrovich calls my name to go in as a guard. As I hit the court, I'm very relieved to see Rick come out for his first rest. I'm going in for Craig, and as my English teacher would say, there's irony in there somewhere. The second I hit the court, my body somehow relaxes and I get into a rhythm. Our point guard is Brent Sands, a terrific dribbler and passer who's very unselfish. Brent steals a pass, and I run with him on a two-on-one fast break. He hits me with a nice bounce pass, I give one right back to him, and he makes the layup.

"Goood, Eeer-nee," Coach yells. "But take shot next time. You open like all-night diner." He's right, but I want to get a little warm before I shoot. I'm playing decently, and a few minutes later, I make my first shot, a twelve-foot jumper from the wing. As the ball swishes through the net with that magical sound, I feel my heart beating faster. I play the entire second quarter and do pretty well, getting a steal and a couple of assists, but no more points. The game gets a little closer with Rick Craig out, and at halftime, we're up by only four.

It's the middle of the third quarter, and I go in again, this time with Rick on the court. I tell myself, *just keep doing what you're doing*. Things are going okay until Rick gets a rebound and I break down court, all alone. Rick leads me with the pass, I catch it, and, five feet from the hoop, dribble the ball off my foot and out of bounds. I run back on defense and don't dare look Rick's way, but I can feel his icy glare. As we move around on defense, I hear him say, "Damn, do you suck."

It's all downhill from there. I throw away a couple of passes, miss a layup, and can't seem to stay with anyone on defense. We go down by five, and Coach P. calls a time-out.

On the way to the bench, Rick turns and grabs me by the jersey. "You're killing us, Choke."

I pull away and try to answer back. "Stop c-c-c-calling me that."

"Then stop p-p-p-playing like that." I'm hating this guy more every minute.

We hit the sideline, and Coach Petrovich settles the team down. It's my turn to sit, and at this point, I welcome the bench. Coach slides up to me. "Eer-nee, what wrong? You playing good, den go eento toilet. You okay?"

I nod that I am, but I'm not.

A few minutes into the fourth quarter, I get back in and manage to run up and down without doing much damage. Rick won't even pass to me now. I sit out the final six minutes and watch as Rick takes over the game, leading the team to a seven-point win. Everyone slaps hands with each other, but Rick totally ignores me. I sit alone at the end of the bench, trying to collect my thoughts.

I'm the last guy to file out of the gym. Tim Sanders is at the door, leaning against the wall. "Nice win."

"No thanks to me."

"Hey. You played pretty well for a while. Then something happened, like something got to you."

No kidding. I do not want any part of this conversation right now. "See you later," I say.

"Hold up, Dolan. Can we talk for a minute?"

"Tim, I really don't want to talk right now."

"Make you a deal," Tim says, picking up a basketball. "If I make a shot from here, you stay for a minute. If I miss, you can split." Tim is standing behind the sideline, at least twenty-five feet from the hoop.

"Okay, take your best shot."

Tim takes off his warm-up jacket and loosens up his

arms. He squares up and launches a high arcing shot that reaches the basket, but rims out.

"So close," I say. I walk out of the gym, take two steps, and stop in my tracks. There was something in Tim's eyes, something so sincere. I walk back into the gym, and Tim is smiling from ear to ear.

"I knew there was something I liked about you, Dolan. Look, there's a lot of camp left, and you can't let one kid ruin your whole time."

"What are you talking about?"

"Nice try. The Craig kid. You're letting him get to you."

"I know, but he's a total dick."

"Yeah, I'd say he's a bit obnoxious. I've seen dozens of kids like him. They have a little game, so they think they're God's gift to basketball and the world. Guys like that love squeezing kids they can squeeze. Don't let him squeeze you, Ernie."

"What am I supposed to do?"

"You have to stand up to him and tell him to lay off."

"You want me to fight Rick Craig?"

"Whoa. Am I running a boxing camp here? No. But guys like that need to be challenged. Show him that there's a real person in there under that jersey."

"I don't know if I can do that. I've got this stutter, and I'll just come unglued."

"I hear you. It's not going to be easy. But not every-thing in life is a layup." Tim picks up another ball and calmly casts a shot from the same spot. The ball arcs higher this time and comes down cleanly through the net. He winks at me and walks out of the gym.

⊕

Our team has won our first two games, but I'm not having a whole lot of fun. I still can't seem to relax when Rick Craig's on the court, and he's on the darn court more than thirty out of forty minutes each game. He still treats me like dirt, and Tim's words of advice are starting to haunt me. Deep down, I know that he's right, but I just can't bring myself to stand up to Craig. I am definitely not a happy camper.

Mike, on the other hand, seems to be having a great time, which, I'm not proud to say, ticks me off a little. He's the star of his team, and they all get along great. He's also making more and more friends outside our cabin. He eats breakfast with me and the roomies, but spends the longer, more social dinner meal at Rick's table with all the cool kids. During our evening free time he hangs with that group, playing pool or air hockey. He tried to include me once, but I don't need to be hit over the head to know I'm not accepted. It's only the third day of camp, and we're already seeing less and less of each other.

After another night of watching Mike's new group from the outside, I walk back to the cabin. I'm all alone, and for the first time ever, I'm feeling homesick. It would be nice to hear a friendly voice, so I decide to call home on my cell.

It'd be easier if my dad had picked up, but my mom answers on the first ring.

"Hi, Mom, it's me."

"Ernie, how are you, dear?"

"Fine, good. . . . Everything's going well." Uh-oh, that didn't sound very convincing.

"You sure? You've never called this early before. You sound a little down." Can't fool her; never could. Now I have to suck it up.

"No, Mom, I'm fine. This place is great. I really like the coaches. . . ."

"And how are the kids?"

"They're good. . . . Nice kids, nice weather . . ."

"How's Mike?"

"He's great. . . . He's waving 'hello' right now."

"Are you eating well, sweetheart?"

"Yeah, Mom, the food's fine. How're Dad and Rusty?" How lame is this? I've never asked about our dog before.

"He's got worms. Rusty, that is." She starts laughing, and I realize how stupid it was to make this call.

"The guys are calling me. I've got to go, Mom. Say hi to Dad."

"Take care, Ernie. Have fun."

What an idiot I am. Now I feel even worse. A while later, Mike enters.

"Hey, E."

"Hey."

"Why'd you split, Ernie?"

"I guess I got tired of watching you guys play ping-pong."

"So instead of sitting there, why didn't you just call 'next game'?"

"Breaking news, Rivers: it's not all that comfortable being around guys who don't want you there."

"What are you talking about, Dolan?"

"I'm talking about your new friends and how they hardly look at me."

"Someone's being a little paranoid."

"Oh, really? Your good friend Rick won't even talk to me, not even on the court. What do you like about that guy, anyway?"

"I don't know. He's smart, funny. He's got game. Rick's really not that bad once you get to know him."

"Easy for you to say. He doesn't call you 'Choke.'"

"Okay, that's not cool, and I've asked him not to do that."

"Yeah, right. Look me in the eye and tell me you asked him that."

"I'm not looking you anywhere. I can't be responsible for how guys talk." Mike's voice rises.

"Yeah, but you don't have to hang with the asshole twenty-four hours a day." My volume increases to match his.

"You can't tell me who to hang with. I like those guys, okay? I can't help it if they don't like you."

"Is that how it is? What happened to the Two Musketeers?"

"You're just jealous because I'm getting a little popular."

"I'm not jealous! Those guys are j-j-j-jerks."

Whoa. I hardly ever stutter when talking to Mike. My stuttering catches him off guard, and we both just stare each other down for a few seconds.

"Did you ever think about trying to fit in a little more?" Mike asks, in a tone I've never heard before.

"Do you ever think about shutting up? I'm the same guy you left home with, Rivers. I may not be one of the best players out there, but at least I'm not a phony."

"You're not a lot of things."

"What the hell is that supposed to mean?"

"You were right, Dolan. You don't belong here."

That hurts. It hurts enough that I completely lose it and throw a wild punch; Mike backs away, and it just grazes his shoulder. He steps closer, with his fist cocked and this crazy look I've never seen before. I don't know who's more surprised by my outburst, me or him. What we both know is that he can pretty much flatten me right now. He just stares at me for a few seconds, which, I swear, is scarier than being hit. Then he suddenly turns on his heel and storms out of the cabin.

So goes our first fight.

7

THE GUY UNDER THE JERSEY

This is so weird. Mike and I, best buds for, like, forever, are not speaking. I take that back. This morning, he did say to me, "Exactly what day are you getting out of the bathroom, dickwad?"

I don't like this. To be more accurate, I hate this. It's so unnatural, and I know it must feel the same to Mike. This stupid thing called "pride" has come between us like a brick wall that went up overnight. Neither one of us will give in and speak to the other, let alone apologize. Okay, I did take a swing at him, but you have to admit, he deserved it. He's the one with the problem, he's the one being an idiot, and he's the one who should apologize.

Mike's totally ignored me for the last twenty-four hours, eating all his meals at Rick's table and dropping by the cabin only to sleep. Albert and Derek have picked up on this, as the tension in the cabin this morning is pretty thick. We're all getting dressed. Mike and I are two feet from each other, but make no eye contact. At one point, I accidentally brush into him.

"Bump into me again, Dolan, and I'm not holding back this time." We just stare at each other.

"Okay, time out," Albert says. "This is totally wack. You two are best friends. You can't do this."

"He's right," Derek chimes in.

"You ladies will have to work this out," Albert says.

"Tell him. You can't even talk to the guy," I say.

"At least I can t-t-t-talk," Mike shoots back.

Ouch. Mike's never put down my stuttering before. This turns the cabin stone-cold silent, and we just stare each other down.

Albert steps in between us. "Guys, when Lindsay Lohan and Hillary Duff had their catfight they just—"

"Shut up, Albert!" Mike and I say simultaneously.

Dead silence again as Albert throws his hands up in frustration. The tension is broken when we hear pounding on the cabin door. Derek opens it to a very excited boy.

"You guys have to come see this."

We grab various shirts and shoes and follow the kid out of the cabin. He leads us up a hilly trail to an area that overlooks the parking lot. Half the guys in camp are gathered around, looking down at a big bus with its hood up, belching smoke as it overheats. Getting off the bus are girls around our age, in all sizes, shapes, and colors.

"They're girls," Derek announces, his mouth wide open.

"Somebody passed biology," Albert says.

"They're definitely girls," Mike says. "But what are they doing here?"

"There's a girls' soccer camp farther up the lake," Derek informs us.

The girls see us watching them and giggle to each other. My eyes scan the gathering of females below. *Whoa, who is that?* She's tall, with long legs and beautiful red hair. While all the others seem to cluster into little groups, this girl sits alone on a large rock and drinks from a bottle of water, and as she does, I can see that even her neck is perfect. She looks up our way, and I could swear she's looking right at me. I smile, but then another girl steps in front of her, ruining our special moment. Okay, *my* special moment.

All the guys descend the hill, to say hi to the girls, I guess. This is something I've never been good at, but I follow them down. Mike and some of the other guys instantly dive in, introducing themselves to girls and making small talk. The really hot redhead is still off by herself, sitting on the rock. If ever I had an opening, this is it. I slowly make my way over to her, and when I'm about twenty feet away, another girl cuts me off. She's got wild, frizzy hair, wears glasses, and is the one person here who seems more nervous than me. She smiles and starts blabbering a mile a minute, like she's stuck in fast-forward mode.

"Hi, I'm Molly, and I'm really shy but my mom says I have to get out of my shell and be more assertive, you know, go up and talk to boys, you're a boy so here goes nothing, I'm in eighth grade and I love horses and modern dance, nod if you like either one of those, guess not, I also like sports, play soccer and I love to go to the Westminster Dog Show, I could go on about dogs forever they're so . . . "

She continues to ramble on and on, and I stand there, nodding my head, even though I can understand only every third word she's blabbing. I'm trying to be polite, but I'm stealing glances toward the redhead on the rock, who, miraculously, is still alone. I've got to get out of here—now.

" . . . but I think Real World is really Fake World, 'cause all the kids know the camera's on them and act accordingly, I am soooo over that show. . . . "

Then, like a gift from heaven, Albert Mann walks up to us. I yank Albert toward me and into the conversation. "Albert, Molly. Molly, Albert. Will you guys excuse me for a minute?" I make my exit, and Molly hasn't missed a beat as she assaults Albert with a ramble about what's on her iPod. I look up, and my dream girl is now being hit on by another boy.

Talk about an opportunity lost. To be honest, I don't know if I would have had the nerve to talk to the redhead or what I would've said, but I've missed my shot, thanks to THE MOST ANNOYING GIRL IN THE WORLD! I find a rock of my own to sit on, or, should I say, sulk on.

A few minutes later, Tim comes out of the office with some engine coolant and pours it into the radiator. The female counselors tell the girls to get back on the bus, and all the guys boo Tim. Albert Mann comes bouncing over to me.

"Ernie, you have no idea what you just did."

"Albert, I'm sorry. I had to get away from her. She was driving me crazy."

"You just made my day, my week, my year! That girl is amazing."

"She is? Yeah, she's something else," I say.

"She has quite a way with words."

"Oh yeah, she uses every one in the dictionary—twice."

"Finally, a girl who can carry on a conversation," Albert says.

"Yeah, but a conversation usually is between *two* people. Did she ever let you talk?"

"Once, but I've heard me talk enough. She's smart, funny, hot, and . . . she loves the Westminster Dog Show! I just put her on my speed dial. Ernie, I think I'm in love!"

"Whatever. I hope you two are very happy together."

"I owe it all to you, buddy." Albert hugs me.

As we walk back to our cabin, I'm thinking that maybe I ought to try to talk to Mike—not to apologize, but to at least try and break the tension a bit. I catch up to him, tap him on the shoulder, and the two of us hang back from the others.

"What's *with* you, man?" I say.

"What's with *you*? You took a swing at me."

"Okay, that was stupid, but tell me you didn't ask for it."

"Look, Dolan, you can't tell me who to hang with. I like meeting new people, okay?"

"Meet whoever you want, Rivers, but those guys are dicks and I don't want to be anywhere near them."

"Fine, then hang with the losers."

"Oh," I say. "So I'm a loser now?"

"*I* didn't call you a loser."

"Right, just like you didn't make fun of my stuttering."

"Okay, that was a cheap shot, but you've got bigger problems."

"Really. And what might those be?"

"You're not fitting in. You're not trying to be one of the guys."

"I don't want to be one of those guys. They're a bunch of conceited phonies. And you're becoming one of them."

"This conversation is so over," Mike says as he stalks off. As I watch him go, I ask myself, *who is this guy*?

⊕

The next day we hit the gym for another game, but it's not just another game. We're playing Mike's team, we're both 3-0, and the winner will sit all alone in first place. I always want to beat Mike, but now I want it more than ever.

Normally, we'd be jawing at each other with playful trash talk and praising each other's good plays, but not today. Today it's all business, as if we're two strangers meeting at the park in a pick-up game.

On top of all the stuff going on with Mike, there's something even bigger on my mind. It's what Tim said. It's time for me to stand up to Rick Craig. I don't know how and when I'm going to do it, but I know I *have* to do it, and it has to be today. I can't get through another game taking Craig's abuse.

It's early in the second quarter, my usual time to enter the game. The first quarter was a back-and-forth battle between the two best players, Rick and Mike. It was actually fun to watch as Mike hit his first three shots, setting the pace. Rick answered back with a spurt of his own, and they each scored eight points. Rick's driving layup at the buzzer put us up by two points.

Coach Petrovich walks along the bench and taps my shoulder. "Eeernie, go een for Scott." I jump up off the bench and get loose, looking for Craig out of the corner of my eye. He's still on the court. I guess Coach P. plans to play him every minute he can. As we take the court, I get the stare. No words, just that chilling look that screams, "Don't dare screw up."

I'm more nervous than ever, not so much about playing, but about doing what I know I have to do. The first time down on offense, I feed Craig with a crisp bounce pass, and he hits a jumper from the free-throw line. "Goood pass, Eeernie!" Coach yells from the bench. I know I'm never going to hear those words from Craig, so I'm happy someone noticed.

At the other end of the court, Mike sets a screen on me and jabs an elbow into my stomach, just to let me know he's there. I respond with an elbow back into his ribs, just to let him know I'm not going anywhere. Mike gets free on the wing and takes a shot that bounces off the rim. I go up for the rebound, and he comes flying in, throwing a shoulder into me and knocking me to the floor. The ref calls him for a foul and gives him a warning. I bounce right up and laugh, pissing him off even more. It's actually getting worse between us. This really gets my adrenaline pumping, and I play harder than ever.

Late in the third quarter, the game is tied when Mike pump fakes Craig off his feet and drives to the hoop. I step in to pick Mike up, and our eyes meet for a second. The determined look on his face says it all. He glides by me with a quick and agile move, going off the glass for the easy layup. Craig is embarrassed, as well he should be.

"Where's the help, Choke? You've got to step up on that."

"Next time, don't let him fake you out of your shorts, Craig." *Did I just say that?* If I'm surprised, the look on Craig's face can best be described as stunned. In fact, when he looks over to me, he takes his eyes off an incoming pass and loses it out of bounds. Now he's even more embarrassed.

My heart is beating out of my chest, and it's not from physical exertion. I don't know exactly where it came from (probably from all the tension with Mike), but my answer back to Craig has stirred something in me. No matter what happens from here, it was worth it just to see that look on his face.

Craig comes out of the game for his usual break. I play decently, making a couple of shots, one over Mike when he switches to guard me off a screen. The rest of us guys do our best, but without Craig in there, we fall behind by six. Mike and the Pacers' talented guard, Jamal King, are putting on a clinic.

Craig re-enters early in the third quarter, and within a few minutes, we're back in the lead. He's hardly passing to me, so I'm not expecting the ball when he drives the lane, gets double-teamed, then hits me with a bullet right under the basket. The ball goes right off my hands and out of bounds. Coach Petrovich calls a time-out, and as we head for our bench, Craig's all over me.

"Get some hands, Choke."

That's it. That's the last straw. I turn right to his face. "Sh-sh-sh-shut up, Craig."

"What'd you say to me?"

"You heard me."

Craig takes a step toward me, and we're now two feet apart.

"Say it again, Choke."

"St-st-stop calling me that."

"Or w-w-w-what?" Craig shoves me.

I shove him back. I don't take my eyes off him. In fact, I don't even blink. But that doesn't mean I'm not scared. The gym has suddenly gone very quiet, and I can sense that everyone is watching. Craig now has his hand in a fist, and he takes another step toward me. He's so close, I can smell him. *Please don't hit me in the mouth. I hate going to the dentist.* Out of nowhere, Coach Petrovich is between us. He grabs both our jerseys and firmly pulls us to the bench.

"What eeze going on heere?"

"I can't play with this guy," I say.

"You can't play at all, Choke. He's killing us, Coach."

"What you just call heem?"

"I called him Choke, because that's what he is."

"You're on a teeem, Craig. My teeem. And on my teeem, we do not call names. You're going to bench for rest of game, and you soospended for next game."

"What?" Craig's voice goes up three octaves.

"You hear me. Seet down!"

Craig looks at me, and then right through me. He kicks the water jug and sits by himself at the end of the bench. Time-out's over, and I go back out on the court.

I'm feeling a lot of things right now, and they're not all good. I'm not one who likes to rock the boat, and now I've capsized the boat. I hate being the cause of any team turmoil, let alone making us lose our best player. On the other hand, I suddenly feel a whole lot lighter, like a huge weight has been lifted from me. I did it. I stood up to Rick Craig and, in Tim's words, showed him the person under the jersey.

The first few minutes after the incident are a daze. I'm running up and down the court, and I see a game in progress, but I can't say I'm actually in it. Our next best player, Brent Sands, is trying to pick up the slack from Craig's absence. By the end of the third quarter, we're down by seven. Coach calls a time-out.

"Come on, guys, stay eeen da game. We can win deez. Heet the boards, and try to run on deez guys when we can. Eeernie, you're playing rest of game, so take your butt out of your head."

"I think you mean my head out of my butt, Coach."

"No difference. Just do it!"

Okay, I may not have the most talent out here, but I can certainly try to give the best effort out here. I deflect a pass and start a fast break. A ball gets loose, and I'm the first one on the floor, diving to grab it. I'll deal with the floor burns later. I hustle on defense and help out my teammates.

We turn things around, cutting their lead to two with a minute to play. But Mike is taking no prisoners today, motivated more than ever by wanting to beat me. Without Craig guarding him, Mike pretty much does whatever he wants. He makes his last four shots, and his team wins by seven. At the end of the game, we go over to the other bench to shake hands with the opposing players. When I come to Mike, he sticks out his hand and barely brushes mine. We don't exchange a word.

Coach P. calls us together and says that despite the loss, he's really proud of the way we played. Brent and a couple of the other guys tell me I played a good game. I head out of the gym and pass Tim, who's standing at his favorite spot against the wall.

"You were something, Dolan."

"I played okay."

"I'm not talking about your play. I mean the way you stood up to Craig."

"Thanks," I say.

With everything going on between Mike and me, I needed a boost, and for the first time since I got here, I feel good about myself.

8
BANANA POWER

The fallout from the incident with Rick Craig is mixed. A couple of guys from the team privately tell me that they're happy I stood up to him, that he had it coming. Three other guys—I guess you can call them Craig clones—resent me for getting him suspended, as if this was my fault. These guys have stopped talking to me, on orders from Craig, I'm sure.

Things don't get any better when we get blown out in our next game, losing by fifteen. We play lousy on both ends of the court, as if we can't get the game over fast enough. And, to be honest, without Craig, our "go to" guy, we're just an average team. We walk off the court, and Craig, who had to watch from the bleachers, is actually smiling as he passes me.

"Are you happy now, Dolan?"

"No. But it looks like you are. You brought this on yourself, Craig. You're the one who hurt this team." He gives me the finger and walks off with his trademark smirk. At least he called me by my name. It's an improvement on "Choke."

Later on, I run into Tim Sanders in the dining hall.

"How's it going, kid?"

"Let's see," I say. "We've lost two straight, and half the team hates me. Do you have any other great advice for me?"

"Yes. Avoid the tuna casserole. It's nasty. Look, Ernie, whatever happens, you did the right thing. And that's going to piss some people off sometimes. Losing games is no big deal. But losing your self-esteem is."

"Yeah, maybe. But I have to face these guys every day. Do you have any idea how mean they can be?"

"Actually, I do. Being fourteen can really suck sometimes."

He's got that right. While the latest situation hasn't made things any easier, somewhere inside myself I *do* feel better. Okay, my self-esteem may not be completely back, but at least it's on the radar screen. I'm not the same kid I was two days ago. I'm a little more relaxed, a little more confident, and I'm starting to feel more comfortable around the other guys.

⊕

I'm in the bleachers, watching Mike's game with Albert, Brent Sands, and a few other boys. We're eating our lunch, and I'm peeling a banana. Mike's team is in a tight game that's going down to the wire.

"They should go back to the zone," Brent says.

"Nah, they're doing fine with man-to-man," Albert replies. Albert snatches my banana and holds it up to my mouth like a microphone. "What do you think, Ernie Dolan?"

"I think I want my banana back." Brent and Albert laugh. Albert has given me an idea, and I now take the banana as my microphone.

"Folks, buckle up, because we're in for quite a ride. Two minutes and eight seconds to play, and the T-Wolves are leading the Pacers by two. Mike Rivers brings the ball up to the front court, eyes peeled for a quick opportunity. Rivers swings a pass over to the kid with the droopy socks. Droopy Socks gives it back to Rivers on a give-and-go, and Rivers goes in for a nifty reverse layup. Mike Rivers has tied the score with a minute, forty to play."

Whoa. Where the heck did *that* come from? Out of nowhere, I just started announcing. The words just seemed to flow right out of me. It was as natural as breathing. And the amazing thing was, as fast as I was talking, I never once stuttered. Brent and Albert look at me and smile.

"That was pretty good, Dolan."

"Give us some more."

"We're tied at forty-seven with fifty-two seconds to play. This is a real nail biter, and I've chewed my last one. T-Wolves working in the frontcourt. Kid With The Buzz Cut dribbles along the baseline, passes it to What's His Name. What's His Name shoots from fifteen and misses by three. Here come the Pacers with a chance to win it. Real Sweaty Guy brings the ball up the court. Forty seconds to play. Folks, if you're not excited about this one, you don't have a pulse.

"The Pacers want to get the rock to Mike Rivers, but Rivers is double-teamed. They're on him like fleas on a dog. Rivers gets a screen, breaks free, and gets a bounce pass at the top of the arc. He's going to run the clock down for the last shot, and everybody in the gym knows it.

"Sixteen seconds, fifteen. Mike Rivers, dribbling with his back to the basket. I've seen that look before, and it means one thing: he's locked in. Rivers working against two defenders with seven seconds to play. Six . . . five . . . Rivers fakes a drive and steps back for an eighteen-footer . . . GOOD! The Pacers win it at the buzzer with a clutch shot from Mike Rivers! And that's how it looked from the cheap seats!"

With that, I take a big bite out of my microphone. Is that laughter I hear? I believe it is. Now I'm hearing applause. I look around to see that the group of kids around me has grown a little larger, all listening to my announcing.

"That was awesome, Ernie."

"You're a natural, man."

"And you're funny."

Are they talking about me? I'm not used to this. Three of the guys clapping are the same guys who stopped talking to me yesterday.

Mike, mobbed by his teammates, eventually breaks away and makes his way over to us. I'm on a roll, so I decide to keep it going. I walk up to him and stick the banana in his face.

"Amazing game, Mike. How did you get that last shot off?" Mike eyes the banana warily. "Just speak into the mike, Mike." Everyone laughs, but Mike remains stone-faced, not playing along. The silence is getting awkward, so I decide to fill in his side of the interview, using my best Mike voice.

"Well, Ernie, when it comes to hoops, I owe it all to you. You taught me everything I know." This cracks everyone up, except Mike, who glares at me and grabs the banana.

"You *wish* you taught me something, Dolan. On that last shot, I knew they expected me to drive to the basket, so I just pulled up and fired. Sometimes they go in, sometimes they don't." I grab the banana right back.

"Well, thanks for sharing that, Mike. Is this guy a master of clichés or what? Great game, Mike. Now, go get a shower. You really need one."

The guys laugh, and even Mike now manages a little smile. As he walks off, he gives me this look that says, "What's gotten into you?" I can't really blame him because, at this moment, I'm wondering the same thing myself.

9

HE WHO
LAUGHS LAST

The mood in our cabin is not quite as tense as it was, although it's hardly normal between me and Mike. My announcing bit during his game might have softened him up a little, but he's still distancing himself from me now that he has his new group of friends.

We're getting dressed to go to breakfast. Mike and Albert are slipping on their basketball shoes.

"Eeewww," Mike says. "There's something in my shoe."

Mike takes his left foot out of his shoe, and it's covered with chocolate syrup. Someone poured the stuff into the front part of his shoes so he wouldn't see it before inserting his foot.

"Crap," he says. "These are my new Nikes. I don't believe this."

"They got me too." Albert has to really work to get his foot out of his shoe. "Glue. They put glue in mine."

Derek and I run to check our shoes. Derek has ketchup in his, and my shoe is lined with maple syrup.

"Great, these are useless," I say.

"We've been pranked, guys," Derek says. "A lot of this kind of stuff went on last year."

A time-honored tradition: the camp prank. It's part of every camp experience, like sunburn and mosquitoes.

"How am I supposed to wear these?" I ask.

"I just want to know who did this," Mike says, his face getting red with anger.

"I've got a pretty good idea," Albert says. "It's probably Craig and his fellow cretins."

"We don't know that for sure. It could've been anybody," Mike says.

"Get real, Mike. I'm sure it was Craig," I say.

Albert stands up and puts his game face on. "It doesn't matter who it was. Whoever did this, they're a bunch of amateurs. No harm, no foul. But now it's ON. We find out who it was, and we pay 'em back, big time."

"I like the way you think, Mann. But how?" Derek wants to know.

"How, you ask? Let me count the ways. Just leave that to me. There's nothing as sweet as payback." The smile on Albert's face is absolutely diabolical. I'm so glad he's on *our* side.

We all walk down to breakfast in sandals and act as if nothing has happened. We don't want to give the perpetrators any satisfaction. But camp pranks have their own code of honor, whereby the pranksters not only have to reveal themselves to their victims, but they also get to revel in it.

Before we even reach the food line, Craig and his roommates walk over to us, smirks all around. Why am I not surprised?

"You guys going to be playing ball in those?" Craig says, eyeing our sandals.

"Why do you care?" Derek says.

"Who said I do?" Craig says. "We're heading over to the gym. I'm sure you guys will 'ketch up' to us." They all laugh.

Another boy says, "You four stick together like glue, don't you?" More laughter.

The three of us look at Mike, who's now more embarrassed than angry. "That was weak, Rick," he says, almost apologetically.

"Yeah, it's old school, Craig," Albert says. "That prank went out thirty years ago."

"Like you've got something better?" Craig answers.

"Most definitely. If I were you guys, I'd sleep with one eye open," Albert says. This shuts Craig up, and he walks off with his posse.

Mike turns to Albert. "Okay, this better be good, Mann, not just another fake rat."

"Don't worry. You're in the presence of the master. Just give me a while to think."

Payback has now become a top priority. Albert disappears for most of the day, and Mike, Derek, and I sit around later that afternoon, trying to come up with juicy payback pranks.

"We can steal all their clothes and throw them into the lake," Mike says.

"Nah, too lame," Derek says. "We need something that really humiliates them."

"I've got one," I say. "We take pictures of them naked and put them on the Internet."

"I don't think so," Mike says. "It's probably illegal, and, hey, do you really want to see any of those guys naked?" He's got a point.

Albert runs into the cabin, completely soaked and covered with mud. He's out of breath and carries a large cardboard box.

"Whoa, it's the Swamp Creature. What happened to you?" I ask.

"Fell in the lake. But it was totally worth it. You guys are gonna love this. Look what the kid just caught."

We gather around the box as Albert slowly opens the

lid. Inside is a large black snake, curled several times around the box. Its head shoots up, and we all jump back in unison.

"That's no fake. Where'd you find it?"

"In the woods near the lake. I had to chase the sucker through the mud. That's when I fell into the water."

"What exactly is it?" Mike asks.

"It's a harmless coral snake, but Craig and those guys won't know that. Especially when it's slithering around inside their cabin."

"I like it," Mike says.

"Dude, that's only the half of it. The snake is just a decoy, just the trigger to a much bigger prank."

"What is it?"

"It's top secret," Albert says. "I can't tell you guys yet. Let's just say it's the perfect payback. But I'm going to need all your help. To pull this off, we have to work together with military precision. You guys just follow my instructions, and I promise this will be big. You in?"

We all look at each other with great anticipation, then back at Albert. Of course we're in.

⊕

Four A.M. Albert wakes the three of us up. He made

us sleep in our clothes, so we're all ready to go. We still have no idea where we're going or what we're doing. Albert is actually wearing camouflage fatigues like some soldier in the jungle. He stands before us, dead serious, speaking in a hushed whisper.

"Okay, men. This is it. Game time, zero hour. I have to warn you, some of you may not make it back."

Mike is losing patience. "Cool it, General, you're freaking us out. Where are we going?"

Albert is enjoying this too much. "You'll see when we get there. Now, grab your cell phones, follow me, and stay together."

We walk slowly and quietly in a single-file line, all following Albert down the dirt paths between cabins. When we pass a cabin window, Albert instructs us to duck down, to avoid being seen. Not much chance of that, since the entire camp is asleep.

We make our way down past the main building and stop in front of the dining hall. Albert huddles us all together.

"Okay, men, listen up. Derek, you stand guard outside the door. You see anyone coming toward this building, text me a warning on my phone. You got that?"

"Yes, sir," Derek answers with an exaggerated salute. Albert motions for Mike and me to follow him inside.

We slip into the dining hall through the open door.

Albert looks around carefully to make sure no one is around, then motions for Mike and me to follow. He tip-toes through the eating area and leads us into the kitchen.

"Let me get the light," Mike says.

"No! No lights. I brought all the light we'll need."

Albert takes out a flashlight and shines it around the kitchen. He takes out two pillowcases and holds them up. "Okay, men. We're going to gather up every gooey, sticky, slippery condiment we can find. Ketchup, mustard, salad dressing"

"So we're gonna put all that crap in *their* shoes?" Mike asks.

"I'm insulted," Albert says. "You don't answer a weak prank with another weak prank. This is going to be huge, trust me. Now, start grabbing stuff."

We all pitch in, grabbing the ingredients Albert asked for and putting them into the pillowcases. Albert grabs two giant rolls of plastic wrap, the kind for packing sandwiches. We work quickly and in silence, with Albert shining his flashlight wherever we need it. All of a sudden, Albert's cell phone beeps, announcing an incoming text message.

"Damn. Someone's coming. Quick, let's hide in here."

We follow Albert into a walk-in freezer and close the door behind us.

"It's freezing in here," Mike says.

"Duh. That's why they call it a *freezer*. Now, keep quiet."

We all stand there shivering, surrounded by meat, chicken, frozen vegetables, and gallons of ice cream. At least we won't starve. After a few minutes, Albert carefully opens the freezer door, and we all strain our necks to look out. Manny, the camp cook, is in the kitchen, preparing to make this morning's breakfast.

"It's the cook. He's gonna be in there all morning. We need someone to distract him. Ernie, go out there and take the guy as far away from this door as you can."

"Me? How?"

"Think of something. Hit him over the head with a zucchini if you have to."

This is crazy. Crazy, but incredible fun at the same time. I watch through the open door as Manny makes his way over to the sink. I slip out of the freezer and stand behind him, several feet away.

"Hi there."

Manny is startled and jumps back. "Ernie! Geez, you scared the hell out of me. What are you doing here at four in the morning?"

That is a very good question, one I do not have an answer for on the tip of my tongue. "Uh . . . I . . . I got hungry, I guess."

"Hungry? Now?"

"Yeah, I think I have a tapeworm or something." Manny looks at me strangely, and then I get an idea.

"Is that a cockroach?" I point to the far corner of the kitchen. Manny quickly makes his way over there.

"A cockroach, in my kitchen? I seriously doubt it."

As Manny bends down to check for the cockroach, I look back to see Albert and Mike slip out of the freezer. Albert gives me the thumbs-up sign as they run out of the kitchen. I start to follow them.

"Where you going, Ernie?" Manny asks. "I thought you were hungry."

"I was . . . but seeing that roach, I lost my appetite."

"There are no cockroaches in my kitchen!"

I shrug and run out. I join the guys outside, and Albert gives me a high five. "Good work, Dolan. Follow me, men."

We proceed single file in the dark, carrying our stolen condiments and trying to be as stealthy as possible. The only sounds come from the crickets and a breeze blowing gently through the pine trees.

We stop about twenty feet from Rick Craig's cabin,

where Albert instructs us to crouch down low. With great pride, he finally reveals the rest of his master plan. He was right; this is going to be good.

First, we line the wooden front porch with the plastic wrap. Working as quietly as possible, using only hand signals, we then pour all of the substances onto the plastic, starting with chocolate syrup, ketchup, maple syrup, and glue, the four surprises we found in our shoes. For good measure, we add two kinds of salad dressing, a dozen broken eggs, and a couple of quarts of cooking oil. The result is a very messy, very fast slip-and-slide.

Now the real work begins. With the small shovels Albert hid in the bushes earlier, the four of us take an hour to quietly dig a three-foot-deep pit in front of the porch. Using a nearby hose, we fill the pit with just enough water to create as much mud as possible. Now all we have to do is wait.

"You're a genius, Mann," Derek whispers.

"Yes, I know."

Albert has thought of everything. Sending out secret invitations, he has invited about half the camp to witness our prank, which will, of course, add to the embarrassment of our victims. At about seven A.M., campers start to arrive, all being as quiet as possible. They've brought video and digital cameras, and gather with us on the lawn a few yards from the mud pit.

Seven-thirty A.M. In accordance with camp ritual, campers are awakened every morning at seven-thirty with soft music piped into their cabins. We hear the music come on. Albert waits a minute, then carries his cardboard box to the cabin window, which is partially open. He carefully opens the lid and pours the snake into the open window. We tiptoe back to watch with our fellow campers.

Voices inside the cabin. Craig and his roommates are awake. Two long minutes go by—nothing. Then, we hear several loud screams.

The cabin door flies open, and Rick Craig is the first one out, looking terrified in his boxer shorts. Rick hits our slip-and-slide and instantly goes down, sliding on his butt right into the mud pit. It's exactly how Albert planned it! Rick is quickly followed by his roommates, who, one by one, all end up on top of each other in the pit.

Cameras go off, and everyone erupts with laughter and cheers. Seems like I'm not the only guy who enjoys seeing Craig get his due.

"That'll teach you guys to mess with the master," Albert announces proudly.

Craig and his roommates are totally embarrassed as they climb over one another to get out of the pit. Craig staggers out, almost unrecognizable as he spits mud from his mouth. He advances menacingly toward Albert. "You are one dead man, Mann." Albert doesn't move, but he's scared—real scared. Just before Craig reaches him, Mike steps between them.

"Chill, Rick."

"Out of my way, Mike."

"Hey, you guys got us first. You're just mad because ours was so much better. You just got out-pranked, man." Mike's the one guy in camp who Craig respects, and he seems to have calmed Craig down for the moment. Craig just stares at the ground in frustration. This is a guy who clearly isn't used to losing, but in this game, he never had a chance.

⊕

I'm in the cafeteria line for dinner with Albert, Mike, and a couple of the other guys who heard me announce yesterday. The line is moving really slowly tonight, and the natives are getting restless. I grab a banana as my microphone and start to wing it.

"I'm here in the cafeteria, where things have come to a grinding halt. Now I can see the reason. At the front of the line is Terry Turley. Turley, six-one, two-fifteen, can put it away with the best of them. Here he goes, folks, loading his plate with roast beef—three slices, four, five.

Turley pivots and goes to his left for the mashed potatoes, a sensational move. He's piling those potatoes so high, you could ski off that mound."

The guys are laughing, so I keep going. I turn to our favorite cafeteria worker, Sam Benson. Benson is a college student from Ohio who's always cracking jokes and giving us extra cookies.

"Folks, meet Sam Benson, one of the most talented guys to ever wear a hair net. Sam, what do you recommend tonight?"

"Burger King."

"You heard it, folks, even the head chef says not to eat here. And there's a good reason: this guy hasn't washed his hands since April." The kids love it, and Sam laughs along with them.

"Hey, you're a natural announcer, Ernie," he says. I don't know about that, but I do know that every time I pick up a banana, I enjoy it more and more.

10

THE GIRLS ARE COMING

Big news: the girls are coming. That's right, we're having a dance with the girls' soccer camp tonight in our gym. They're being bused over here as I speak. When the dance was announced this morning at breakfast, the entire dining hall erupted with whoops and cheers. You would think we'd all spent our whole lives on a desert island and never had contact with anything female. Wait—in my case, that's almost true.

Here's the thing about me and girls: there's something about them that makes me a little anxious. Okay, very anxious. Intellectually, I know girls are just like guys, only with a few different body parts, but when I get around them, weird things happen. It's like something possesses my body. Being shy and afraid I'm going to stutter, I feel intimidated and start to freeze up. I find it impossible to make eye contact, so I adjust my gaze about a foot lower, which usually has me staring at their chest. I finally realized this was not a good focal point after being slapped by Nancy Prior in homeroom. Since then, I have adjusted my gaze and now concentrate solely on the girl's forehead. This usually brings a response like "Do I have something in my hair?" Hey, it's better than being slapped.

The thing is, I've been thinking about that mysterious redhead ever since I saw her. I wonder what she looks like up close. I wonder what she smells like. I hope I'm not disappointed. I really would love to talk with her, maybe even dance with her. I've been deep-breathing all day to try and calm myself for the challenge ahead. I so wish I was Mike, at least for tonight. Mike knows how to talk to girls, make eye contact in the right place, and even knows how to flirt. He's actually had a couple of dates and has gone over to girls' houses. Right now, I figure I'm about ten years away from that.

Friday, seven forty-five: fifteen minutes until the big event. Four boys, one bathroom, one mirror: it's not a pretty sight. Albert Mann has been in the shower for the last half hour, and I still have to use it.

"Come on, Albert, you've been in there, like, forever," I say.

"Sorry, but I haven't showered since Tuesday."

"That's too much information," Mike says. Mike

nods to me. "I know how to get him out." Mike goes into the bathroom and sticks his hand into the shower, turning off the hot water. Albert shrieks and runs out of the shower, still soapy.

"That's cold, guys, that's *really* cold."

"You're worse than my sisters, Mann," Mike says.

"You guys are just jealous because I have a girl waiting for me. You're all gonna have to take your chances."

"Albert, when you talked to Molly those ten times, did you ask her who that redhead is?"

"Yes, but she hasn't met her yet. She says the girl is kind of a loner and stays to herself."

"You're a lot of help." I hurry up and get into the shower, but there's hardly any hot water left. I scrub all the important areas, get out, and start to throw on some clothes.

Seven fifty-five. The four of us scurry around the small cabin like rats trying to find their way out of a maze. We're all trying to get dressed, deal with our hair and spray as much good-smelling stuff on ourselves as we possibly can.

"Does this shirt make me look chubby?"

"You *are* chubby."

"Pass the deodorant."

"Should I gel or spike?"

"Who's got a belt I can borrow?"

"Great, I've got a zit the size of Montana."

"Hey, that's my comb!"

"How's my breath?"

"Get away from me."

"Does anyone know how to dance?"

"Dance? I can barely speak."

"Crap, I just sprayed Lysol under my arms." That was Albert, but considering his shower schedule, Lysol is exactly what he needs.

Eight o'clock. We all push each other away to take one last look in the mirror.

Derek says, "Bring on the girls."

"We *are* the girls," I say, as we all laugh.

⊕

The gym is almost unrecognizable. I can't believe it's the same sweaty, smelly place we play in every day. The baskets have been raised up, and nice decorations cover the walls. Tables are set up with popcorn, pretzels, chips, candy, and soda. Two boys act as DJs, playing CDs for dancing. Tim and Laurie are there, along with several of the coaches. At the door, everyone is issued a name-tag, which we write our first name on, then stick to some part of our clothing. Coach Petrovich comes up to us and looks us over.

"Looooking gooood, boys. Should shower more often." He winks, then joins the other coaches in the corner. As I look out across the gym, the girls congregate on one side, the boys on the other. It reminds me of this Discovery Channel show I saw where rhinos stalked each other before mating. The only difference is that these mammals are whispering, giggling, and pointing, and most of them smell a lot better.

Some of the more aggressive guys are already venturing across the floor toward the girls' side. Mike and Derek join them, and I'm standing with Albert, who's looking around for Molly. Molly weaves through several people, almost knocking one poor guy over, then runs up to Albert, giving him a big hug.

"I missed you."

"I missed you too."

"Geez," I say, "you guys have only known each other for ten minutes."

"Yes, but it was the best ten minutes of my life," Albert says.

"You smell so good," Molly says to Albert. "What is that fragrance?"

"Lysol." Molly laughs, thinking Albert's kidding.

"So, where's that redhead you want to meet?" he asks.

"I don't know." I look around the gym. Molly yanks me by the shirt and points across the floor.

"She's over there, in the green dress, not my color, but it works on her, you should totally go over and talk to her, as my mom always says, 'nothing ventured, nothing gained,' you're pretty cute, okay, you're no Brad Pitt, but you have nice hair and . . . "

"Let's get some food," Albert says, pulling her away. I feel like I've been saved from an attack dog. So here I am, completely on my own. Mike and Derek are already dancing with girls, and Albert is minutes away from making wedding plans. I survey the gym, and there she is, standing about forty feet away, talking to a couple of other girls.

I walk cautiously, remembering the Discovery Channel show and how some rhinos were gored. I make my way over to the food table and grab a handful of M&Ms. I'm counting on the sugar rush to give me courage. I slowly walk toward the drink table, and now I'm only ten feet away from her. Wow. She's taller than I thought and much prettier up close. Now I'm really nervous. There's no way I'm comfortable enough to just go right up to her, so, like some of the smarter rhinos, I decide to approach from behind.

I casually make my way to the other side of the drink table. "Red" is talking to another girl and has her back to me. I position myself so I can try to read her name-tag without, of course, looking like I'm trying to read her name-tag. She turns, and I take a quick peek, picking up the letters: I-Z-Z-I-E. Then she actually looks at me, and I'm so nervous, I don't even find it strange that this girl has the same name as my Dad's auto mechanic. It's now or never.

"Hi, Izzie, I'm Ernie."

"The name's Lizzie." She hits the "L" hard, pointing to the one letter I missed. Good start. I feel like a complete idiot, and I know from experience that I have to recover quickly. I need a killer comeback, and I need it right now.

"Cool braces."

"Braces are so *not* cool. I hate my braces." This was not quite the killer comeback I was going for. Her girlfriend laughs, and Lizzie with an "L" starts looking around the room. "Do you want something?" she says, not in a bad way, but just wondering. I do want something, of course. I want to dance with her. Maybe even talk to her and get to know her a little. I've come this far, so I may as well go for it.

"W-w-w-would you like t-t-t—" I can't get the rest out. Lizzie just stares at me with this look of pure pity.

Just then, another boy, one who actually speaks English, walks over to her and asks her to dance. He leads her away by the hand to the dance floor.

I'm sweating, starting to hyperventilate, and my knees are buckling. I have to sit down, right now. I plop down on the end of the drink table, and the force of my weight actually flips the other end of the table. Several big bottles of soda are catapulted into the air and end up soaking two girls nearby. By the way, the sound of two teenage girls screaming is a lot louder than I ever imagined. It's loud enough to stop the entire room and call everyone's attention to me.

"You idiot!"

"Thanks a lot, you dork!"

"Sorry," I mutter. I pick myself up and try to locate the door, but now the room is spinning. I end up losing my balance and start grabbing for something to hold on to. Unfortunately, what I grab is the cardboard "Welcome" sign. The sign is attached to other decorations, and I end up pulling down a whole string of them, several of which land on other kids.

"What's wrong with this guy?" People are laughing and staring, and this is, hands down, the worst moment of my life. Avoiding everyone's eyes, I sprint for the door.

I'm outside now. I'd be great if I could just catch my

breath. I find a bench and collapse onto it. I feel totally humiliated. What's wrong with me? Am I ever *not* going to be a geek around girls?

I catch my breath and calm down enough to start walking. I'm not sure exactly where I'm going, but I've got to stay outside in the fresh air. Without even realizing it, I end up down at the lake. I sit down in one of the row-boats and stare out at the water, which is illuminated by a full moon.

A few minutes later, I'm six years old again. I'm playing with my Legos in the living room as the smell of my mom's chocolate chip cookies wafts in from the kitchen. I'm building the coolest castle ever, with a great big moat that no one can penetrate. I'm inside that castle, and I'm completely safe. Safe from girls, safe from bullies, safe from trying to be like everyone else. The memory brings a smile to my face. Then it hits me. Who am I kidding? I may have been safe then, but I'll never be safe again.

I just never thought that *I'd* be the dangerous one. That I'd be tripping over my own self like that.

Now I'm crying. I haven't done this since—since, like, forever. Tears are running down my cheeks, and I'm sobbing like, well, like a six-year-old.

"Ernie." Someone's calling. Great. I sniffle back a

few tears and start wiping my eyes. "Ernie, what are you doing out here?" I turn around to see Tim standing a few feet away.

"I came here to be alone. That's a hint, Tim."

"Yeah, I got that. But I'm not leaving."

"Then I'm going to jump in, and I may not come back up."

"That would be a tragedy. I'd have to jump in after you, and these are new pants."

"Is this funny to you? Didn't you catch my performance in there?"

"I saw the very end of it. I'm sorry, Ernie. I know it was embarrassing."

"Embarrassing? No, it was humiliating!" Tim climbs into the other end of the rowboat and is facing me. "And get your own rowboat, will you?"

"Sorry. But I'm not leaving until you tell me what happened."

"You want to know what happened?" I'm almost shouting now, so I take it down a couple of notches. "What happened was I blew it, Tim. I blew it big time. I tried to ask this girl to dance, and I completely froze up."

"Okay. But, news flash: you're not the first guy to do that. Women have this strange power over us."

"It was much worse than that. I called her by the

wrong name, pointed out her braces, then I stuttered. . . . Boy, did I stutter. I totally choked."

"You didn't choke."

"That's exactly what I did. I'm a choker, Tim. Maybe Rick Craig is right. When the game's on the line or when I face a pressure situation, I totally lose it. I choke."

"Whoa, Ernie, stop. We're talking about girls here. Girls turn guys into Jell-O. That's why they're girls, man."

"Then why is it so easy for the other guys? Sports, friends, girls. They're not freezing up. They're not stuttering."

"I know it looks that way, but it really isn't. Every boy in this camp is dealing with something."

"Not every boy. Look at Craig," I say. "I hate him, but you know what? For just one day, I'd like to be that guy. Not the obnoxious guy, but that confident guy, the guy who steps up in the clutch, the guy everyone wants to hang with. Just once, I'd like to be like that. Be The Man."

"I know you can't see it right now, but your time's gonna come. But before you can be 'The Man,' you have to be you. You've got to find the real Ernie Dolan in there, and let him out."

"Come on, Tim. What if this is just who I am?"

"It's who you were tonight. But it's not who you're going to be."

"How do you know?"

"Because I was a lot like you at fourteen."

"Please don't bullshit me. You ride a motorcycle and have, like, the hottest wife. No offense."

"Yeah, *now*. I'm pushing thirty, kid. But when I was your age, I was a mess. I stuttered too, and much worse than you."

This stopped me cold. "You stuttered?"

"Oh yeah, big time, as you would say. I once had to recite the Gettysburg Address, and it took me thirty minutes. Lincoln's still rolling over in his grave. And that's not all. When I got near a girl . . . I would be so nervous, I would hum."

"You'd hum?"

"Yes. Because I was afraid I'd stutter. Girls would ask what song I was humming. Look, embarrassing, even humiliating things happen, but you have to move on. Life's more like basketball than you think. You make mistakes, but you have to keep playing. And, there are moments in life, just like in basketball, where an opportunity is going to present itself. That's when you have to believe in yourself and take your best shot, because you may never have that shot again."

"How do you know so much, man?"

"I don't. But I do know this. You're going to do great things, Dolan."

I look into his eyes and wonder why this virtual stranger has so much confidence in me.

"You like Rocky Road ice cream?" Tim asks.

"I love Rocky Road ice cream."

"Well, we just got a special order in that we're supposed to serve for dessert tomorrow night. In all good conscience, I can't let the campers eat an ice cream that hasn't been taste-tested. I could use some help with that."

I smile. Never thought I'd do that again.

11

THIS IS NO GAME

It's after midnight, and as tired as I am, I still can't sleep. As much as I try to get it out of my mind, I keep replaying my meltdown at the dance four hours ago. Thank goodness for Tim, who was there for me . . . again. He's the coolest adult I've ever met, and I'm lucky to have someone like him to talk to. The roommates were okay about the incident; at least they didn't tease me or anything. Only Albert actually saw everything that happened, and he was pretty sympathetic. Derek and Mike didn't really talk to me about it, other than to ask if I was okay.

A little while later, Albert and Derek are in a deep sleep, and Albert is snoring loudly. I hear Mike rustling up in the bunk above. He carefully climbs down and pulls on a T-shirt in the darkness. He slips on his tennis shoes and heads for the door.

"Mike, where you going?"

"Nowhere. Just getting some air."

"I can't sleep, either. Can I come with you?"

"No. Just go back to bed, Ernie. I'll be back in a while."

Mike slips out the door, and I get this funny feeling. I know he's up to something, but I don't know exactly what. Even though we're back to talking to each other, things haven't been the same since our fight. There's definitely a strain there.

This isn't the first time he's snuck out at night to hang with Craig and his posse. I hate not being best buds like we used to be. Part of me says to forget it and just let him go. But there's this other part of me, the part that has to know where he's going. I quickly throw on some sweats and shoes, grab a flashlight, and tiptoe out of the cabin.

The summer night air is still warm and sticky. With hardly any moon and all cabin lights out, the woodsy area is totally dark. The only sounds I hear are the crickets and an occasional animal scurrying through the brush.

Mike got a pretty good head start. I shine my flashlight in several directions until I pick him up. He's heading away from the cabins toward the lake. I quickly turn off the light, not wanting to let him know I'm here.

I start out in his direction, using my flashlight to illuminate only the ground before me. I walk slowly and carefully, because the trail is full of thistles and big boulders.

More than once, I stub my toe and have to stop myself from screaming out in pain. I can just make out Mike's image as he winds his way down the trail. It helps that he's wearing a white T-shirt.

Mike nears the lake and heads for a small shed with a light on. I hang back behind a tree and watch as he reaches the shed, looks around to make sure no one sees him, and goes inside. I hear the faint sound of distant voices greeting him.

Leaning against the tree for a few minutes, I realize that the sound I'm hearing is my rapid breathing. When we were little, Mike and I pretended we were spies and spied on our parents and other kids. And now here I am, spying on him for real. I feel weird about it, but I know whatever Mike's up to can't be good.

I walk toward the shed and see there is a small window on one side. I get down and crawl around to a point right under the window. Standing up at my full height, the window is still too high for me, so I find a large log to stand on. I slowly rise up to the window and peer in. It's some kind of storage shed, full of gardening tools, boxes of supplies, and large containers of cleaning fluids.

I hear voices, but don't see anyone. Then, standing up a little taller, I get a better look. Mike is there with a boy named Jake Tinsley and Rick Craig. The three of them are smoking cigarettes and taking swigs from a bottle of vodka. My stomach sinks. I'm not that naïve. I know some kids our age drink, but this isn't just any kid—it's Mike. I hate Rick Craig and the influence he has over my friend. But, at the same time, I hate Mike too. No one is forcing him to do this. It's his decision to drink.

Now what? I'm really not sure what to do. It's Mike's life, and I'm certainly not his father. But I am his best friend (or used to be), and I don't want to see him get hurt in any way. He's doing something stupid, and as his best friend, I feel it's my duty to try to stop him. If I were doing something stupid, wouldn't I want Mike to bail me out? Then again, he's been kind of a dick lately, so why should I give a damn about what he does? But there's all this history between us—all those years, all those best-friend moments.

All of that races through my mind as I knock on the shed door, unsure of what I'm going to say. The door opens a crack, and Craig's face is behind it.

"What do you want, D-D-D-Dolan?"

"I want to talk to Mike."

"Mike doesn't want to talk to you. Go away."

"Let him in, Rick," I hear Mike say. I push past Craig and step into the shed. Mike looks at me and shakes his head. "I can't believe you followed me down here."

"What are you doing, Mike?"

"Don't worry about what I'm doing, okay?" He's already a little high, slurring his words. "Want a drink, Ernie?"

"I don't want him here," Craig says. "He won't drink with us anyway. He's a wimp."

Mike gets up and stumbles over to me with the vodka bottle in his hand. "Here, E, show him you're not a wimp." Mike hands me the bottle. All eyes are on me, like I'm some kind of rat in a lab experiment. I take a long look at the bottle of vodka. It'd be so easy right now to just take a swig and shut these guys up. Too easy. But I have nothing to prove to them.

"No thanks," I say.

"What did I tell you, Mike? He's a wuss."

"Come on, Mike," I say. "Come back to the cabin with me. This is stupid, man."

"What are you, my mother?" The other guys laugh, and it's at that moment I know I've lost him. "You want to be a friend, Ernie? Just leave, will you?" The disgust in his voice says it all.

"You're a bigger idiot than I thought, Mike."

"You heard him, get out of here," Craig says. "And Dolan, you tell anyone about this, you're gonna wish you didn't." With that, Craig pushes me out the door, closing it in my face.

I hike back to our cabin, feeling sick to my stomach and totally confused. Maybe I should have been more forceful. But what I'm really thinking is that I shouldn't have followed Mike in the first place. The look on his face when he told me to leave was one I've never seen before. I couldn't care less if Rick Craig hates me, but I really don't want to lose my best friend forever.

By the time I get back to the cabin, I'm just angry. I tried to help Mike, and he threw me out. Screw him. I guess, above everything else, I'm disappointed.

It's weird how you think you know someone, but then you really don't. When I think about it, Mike's always been the one who loves to follow the crowd, especially the "cool" crowd. I stare at the cabin ceiling and wonder if this is going to be the end of our friendship. Mike's going to go back to school and start hanging with all the wrong people, and that'll be it for us. We'll pass each other in the hall and nod, just two guys sharing the same space, but certainly not friends anymore.

Three fifteen A.M. I must have dozed off for a couple of hours, but now I'm wide awake. I'm suddenly overcome by this horrible sense of worry. It's just a feeling I have. There's no way I'm going to sleep another minute, so I get up, put on a sweatshirt and some shoes, and go outside.

The first thing that hits me is this faint smell of smoke, kind of like a barbecue, but not really. I walk toward the lake, and the smell gets stronger. Then, coming through the trees, I see it: a bright orange glow. It's the kind of glow that can only come from a fire.

Quickly making tracks toward the lake, I realize what's burning. It's the storage shed.

I scream at the top of my lungs. "Fire! Fire by the lake! Help! Fire!" I notice several cabin lights going on, but I can't wait for help. I run as fast as I can down the trail to the storage shed. From fifty yards away, I can already feel the heat, and with every step I take, it gets hotter.

I reach the shed and stop in my tracks, almost numb at what I'm seeing. One whole side of the shed is burning, along with part of the roof. Bright orange embers are shooting into the sky, and smoke is everywhere. I see a figure stumbling out of the shed. It's Jake Tinsley, completely disoriented. He's shaking, coughing, and crying all at once.

"Jake, is Mike still in there?" Jake falls to the ground, coughing. All he can do is nod. I walk closer to the shed door, and the temperature rises a hundred degrees. I try to look inside, but the smoke is too thick to see anyone. I yell into the shed: "Mike! Mike, get out of there!"

No response. I try yelling louder: *"Mike! Mike! Miiiiiike!"*

After an agonizing minute, I hear coughing, then see a figure moving. It's Mike, crawling out on all fours. I run over to him and help him up.

"Mike, it's Ernie. Are you okay?"

Mike coughs, trying to get a breath. His sweatshirt is singed, and he has black soot all over his face. I touch his shoulder, but it's as hot as an oven and I immediately jerk my hand away. Mike takes a few deep breaths of fresh air, shakes his head clear, and finally recognizes me.

"Ernie. Fell asleep. Then it got really, really hot. Then . . . I heard you calling my name." He coughs violently.

"You're not burned, are you, Mike?"

"Don't think so. But Rick . . . he's still in there. He got drunk and passed out. I tried to get him out, but . . ." Mike buries his face in his hands.

People are starting to arrive at the scene. Tim and Laurie appear, along with several coaches and more and more campers, some half dressed. There's a common look on everyone's face—shocked disbelief. Voices are shouting, and people are running around in different directions. It's the definition of pure chaos.

"Someone get a hose. And hurry!"

"Call 9-1-1!"

"Is there anyone else in the shed?"

Laurie and Tim tend to Mike and Jake, laying them down on the ground and looking them over.

My attention returns to the shed. Several of the coaches are approaching cautiously. Rick Craig is in there, passed out. Is he even alive? The fire has now lapped around most of the walls and a good part of the roof.

I walk back closer to the shed, and the heat is even more intense. I crouch down and, through the flames, notice a little pocket near the door that isn't burning—yet. I really don't think about it. I don't weigh any options, and I don't consider any consequences. I just know there's a kid in there who is going to die. I can do this. I have to go for it.

I flop on my stomach and crawl furiously toward the shed door. As I reach the door, voices are screaming at me: "Ernie, get away from there!" "Come back here!" Someone actually grabs at my ankle, but misses.

I'm inside. I can't believe how hot it is. My face and hands feel like they're in an oven, and I'm already gushing sweat from every pore in my body. I think to myself, this is what it must feel like on the sun. There's this strange popping sound, the sound of hot embers flying around. A couple of them hit me, and I instinctively flick them off.

Even more dangerous, parts of the ceiling are falling in, and I have to roll out of the way to dodge them.

Through the smoke, I see Rick Craig's motionless body on the floor. Flames are closing in on him. I try to keep my face down to avoid the smoke, but I can already feel it burning my lungs. I keep crawling.

I reach Rick's basketball shoes. They're melted onto his feet like a grilled cheese sandwich. I grab a hold of the hot, sticky rubber and start to pull. Man, is he heavy. He must outweigh me by forty pounds, and right now, he's what they call dead weight. I hope that's just an expression. Drawing as much air into my lungs as I can, I start to pull Rick out, inch by inch. My arms feel like they're being ripped out of their sockets, but I keep on pulling. A burning ember falls on my shirt, and I feel a sudden sting of pain.

I turn my head to avoid the smoke and see a shelf full of cleaning fluids. All I know is, whenever I read those labels, the one word that screams out is "flammable." Any one of those containers can explode any second.

I pull harder and faster, using every ounce of strength I have left. All of a sudden, I feel someone pulling my feet. I've actually reached the door, where Tim and Coach Petrovich are each pulling me by the ankles as I drag Rick.

The next thing I know, Coach is carrying me while Tim and a couple of others pick up Rick and carry him out. I'm coughing up soot and can't seem to get a breath.

Someone takes a blanket and smothers the smoldering embers on my sweatshirt.

They lay me on the grass, and someone else comes over and puts an oxygen mask on my face. The rush of oxygen is cold and has an odd smell. Within seconds, I'm breathing normally again.

"Ernie, are you all right?" It's Tim, leaning over me, looking very worried. I try to get an answer out, but my throat burns and it's too hard to talk.

"Ernie, do you know who I am?" I nod. "How many fingers am I holding up?"

I hoarsely mutter, "Three." I try to get up, but I'm dizzy from all the smoke and my legs are like rubber.

"Stay down, kid. There's no hurry."

I'm shaken up, and my arm muscles are burning like crazy, but I'm really okay. A minute later, I sit up and look a few yards to my left and see that Rick Craig isn't so lucky. He's unconscious. Several people are gathered around him as Laurie starts performing CPR. She's a nurse, so I'm sure she's done this a lot, and she's the coolest and calmest one out here.

"He's breathing," Laurie says, "but he's still unconscious. We've got to get him to a hospital."

Rick's hair is all singed, and his skin is burned in several places. The scariest thing is that he looks lifeless, like a rag doll. We hear sirens in the distance as fire trucks and paramedics approach.

The next noise is the most frightening thing I've ever heard. Something inside the shed explodes, blowing out what's left of the walls and collapsing the roof.

Within seconds, the entire shed disappears. Everyone watches in stunned silence as the smoldering remains of the shed light up the night sky, coloring it in yellow and orange streamers. It's the scariest fireworks show I've ever seen. Some kids are crying; others have to be consoled by counselors.

Several coaches carefully put Rick on a stretcher and carry him up to the parking lot, where the ambulance has just arrived.

I feel strong enough to stand up. I see Jake Tinsley and Mike talking to Laurie. They seem to be okay, just really shaken up. Laurie now walks over to me.

"How are you doing?"

"I'm okay, I think."

Laurie shines a light in my eyes and examines my skin for burns. "Take a deep breath for me." I try, but I start coughing again. "That was an amazing thing you did, Ernie Dolan." She gives me a big hug.

Coach Petrovich comes up to me. His face is pale, and he looks scared. "You're someteeng, keed. Dat's bravest teeng I ever see."

Kids come up to me, some patting me on the back, others shaking my hand, some just staring at me in awe. Someone utters the word "hero." I don't get it. Maybe it hasn't sunk in, but I don't feel like I did anything special. Right now, I don't feel anything. I'm completely numb. Tim walks over to me.

"You sure you're okay?"

"Yeah, I'm fine."

"Dolan, yesterday when I gave you my little speech about taking your best shot, I didn't mean for you to run into a burning building. How . . . why . . . what the hell made you do that?"

"I don't know," I say. And I really don't. At the moment, it doesn't even seem real. It's as if all this is happening to someone else, and I'm just watching it.

Then I see Mike shivering off to the side and go over to him. There is something in his eyes I've never seen before. It's pure fear.

"You all right, Mike?"

"Yeah, I think so. Thanks to you. You were incredible. Weren't you scared in there?"

"I don't know. I'm sure I was. I just didn't have time to think about it."

"You've got more guts than anyone I've ever seen."

"I just reacted, Mike. You would've done the same thing."

"No, I wouldn't."

"Sure you would."

"I wouldn't!" Why is he yelling at me? "Don't you see? I never tried to get Rick out. I just said I did. The second I saw Jake run out, I crawled right out after him. It was so freaking hot, and I couldn't breathe. I left Rick there to die. I'm a coward."

Mike starts crying, really sobbing. I've only seen him like this once, when we were six and his dog died.

There's nothing I can say to him at this moment. So I do the only thing a best friend can do. I give him a hug. Mike hangs on like he's never going to let go.

12
THE DAY AFTER

I wake up and realize I'm in a strange place. I look at the clock and see that it's nine-thirty A.M. I'm lying on a cot next to Mike and Jake in a back room of the camp office. Laurie insisted that the three of us sleep in the camp infirmary so she could check on us during the night. As exhausted as I was, it was hard to get to sleep after everything that had happened, but I remember zonking out about five A.M. Laurie woke me at least once to check my blood pressure. I look at myself in a mirror and hardly recognize the guy staring back at me. Some of my hair is singed, and all the color has been drained from my face.

I tiptoe out of the room and make my way into the office. Laurie is there, drinking a cup of coffee.

"Hey, you. How are you feeling?"

"Okay. Just tired."

"Yeah, well, you had a busy night. Sit down. I want to check you out."

Laurie takes my blood pressure again and listens to my chest with her stethoscope. As I sit there, I think back to the first day of camp when I remarked how hot this woman was in front of her husband, and how Tim said, "You better stay out of the nurse's office, because I'll be watching you, Dolan." I smile as I remember it.

"What's so funny?" Laurie asks.

"Nothing."

Laurie takes a weird-looking device and asks me to breathe into it, taking in the biggest breath I can. I take a deep breath and watch a little red ball rise up in a plastic cylinder. Then I start coughing.

"That was pretty good. You've still got some smoke in your lungs, but it'll clear up soon. All in all, I'd say you are one lucky boy."

"I know. What about Craig?"

"Tim was with him at the hospital. He's conscious, but he's got some second-degree burns and a bad case of smoke inhalation. He's going to be okay, thanks to you."

Mike and Jake wake up and go through their examinations. They're okay, all things considered.

There's an all-camp meeting at ten-thirty, so Mike and I head down to the cafeteria for some breakfast.

Mike seems to be in another world. He's walking really slowly and stares straight ahead like he's in some kind of zombie trance.

"Mike, what is it? What's up with you?"

"I don't know. I can't stop thinking about last night. Can't get it out of my mind. The flames, the heat. It's a miracle we all didn't die in there. I'm so lucky, Ernie. And so stupid." He coughs.

"You're not stupid."

"Going into that shed. . . . I can't believe I let Craig suck me in like that. How could I think that guy was so cool? You were right about him all along."

I can't argue with that, but this is not the time to say "I told you so."

"Okay, you screwed up, but the main thing is you're all right."

"Thanks to you. I was asleep in there, and I never would've woken up if you hadn't called my name. You saved my life, E." He looks like he's going to cry again.

"Nah. I just woke you up, man. I've always been good at waking you up." This brings a little smile to his face. "C'mon, let's get some breakfast. I'm starved."

Mike and I walk into the cafeteria, and it's not the same boisterous place we know. The first thing that hits me is the eerie quiet. The usual sounds of music, laughter, and raised voices are gone. We pass a few of the kids, and they all have that same numb look. It's that look you get when you see a bad accident. And last night was a very bad accident.

A few kids are talking, but when I walk in, the room suddenly goes silent. I look around and see everyone looking at me, a couple of them pointing. A few guys come up to me.

"Way to go, Dolan."

"You are one brave dude, Ernie."

"You saved his life, man."

"What was it like in there?"

"You're a hero."

This is strange and, I must admit, a little uncomfortable. It's all too fresh and still unreal in some way. How do you respond to this? I just say "thanks" and try to get through my cereal.

"What's up with all that?" I ask Mike.

"They're just reacting to what you did, E. Go with it."

A while later, we're all in the gym. It's so quiet you could hear a pin drop. All of the coaches and counselors are lined up in chairs behind a podium, along with four strangers. I've never seen so many serious faces in my life.

Tim and Laurie walk in, and Tim goes up to the podium.

"I spent last night at the hospital with Rick Craig, one of your fellow campers. He's going to be okay, but he is very lucky to be alive. Now, I'm not going to stand up here and lecture you guys on drinking. Last night was a big enough lesson—one that none of us will ever forget. But today will not be camp as usual. We're suspending all games and activities. Today is the day for everyone to reflect on what happened last night and to talk about it."

Tim introduces us to the four strangers. They are a crisis team of psychologists Tim and Laurie brought in to help us deal with what happened. Tim says they're here for anyone who feels he needs to talk about the fire and its aftermath. He makes it mandatory for Mike, Jake, and me, the guys who were inside the burning shed, and sets us up with the very first sessions.

I'm ushered into a small back office in the main building, and I'm feeling uncomfortable already. I don't want to be here; I really don't want to talk to some stranger about what happened and how I feel. The truth is, I'm not sure just how I feel because I haven't exactly had a lot of time to think about it. I feel even more uneasy when the guy I walk in to see is a woman.

"Hello, I'm Linda Malone. Nice to meet you, Ernie."

I shake her hand and nervously take a seat in the chair facing her.

"First of all, how are you? How are you feeling?"

"Fine. Good. I have a little trouble taking a real deep breath, but that's getting better."

"Good to hear," Linda says. "That was quite an act of bravery you performed last night."

"Yeah, I guess. At least that's what some people are saying."

"I hear one of the boys you saved was your good friend, right?"

"Yeah, Mike Rivers."

"And one of the boys . . . you had some trouble with him, didn't you?"

"Rick Craig. Oh, just a little."

"And what was the nature of the trouble?"

"He just got on me a lot."

"Physically?"

"No, he just ragged on me a lot. What does this have to do with anything?"

"I'm just trying to understand who was in that shed. Ernie, have you thought at all about why you did this?"

"Not really. I haven't had much time to think about anything."

"You know, there aren't a lot of people who would have done what you did—run into a burning building."

"Geez, you say it like what I did was a bad thing."

"Not at all. What you did was heroic and completely selfless . . . but it was at great risk to yourself. You could have been hurt or even killed."

"I guess I didn't stop to think about that."

Linda looks at me and nods. I'm not sure what she's getting at, but these shrink people have hidden motives and meanings. She's starting to get annoying.

"I've never gone inside a burning structure to save someone, and quite frankly, I don't know if I ever could. I'm just wondering why you would put yourself in such danger."

Now she's *really* getting annoying. "I didn't think about the danger. I just did it. You think I tried to off myself?"

"No. But I can't help but wonder if you were trying to prove yourself in some way."

"To who?"

"You tell me. Your peers? Maybe to yourself?"

"No offense, Ms. Malone, but do you think I went into a fire on purpose to show off?"

"I didn't say that, Ernie. I'm just trying to get an idea of your mind-set when you went into that burning shed."

My mind-set? Give me a freaking break. She's driving me out of my mind-set.

"Look, I'm kind of wiped out. Can I go now?" I ask.

"Sure. You take care of yourself. You did an amazing thing, Ernie."

I walk out of there, angry and confused. The lady asked too many stupid questions that all had obvious answers. I don't think I was trying to prove anything to anyone. But if in some weird psychological way I was, so what? The important thing is that a couple of kids are alive because of me, and it doesn't really matter much why.

I meet up with Mike a while later, and he's much more like his old self.

"That psychologist guy was really nice. He told me not to feel guilty about what I did. Said I was in the wrong place at the wrong time and I should just be thankful to be okay. How did it go with you?"

"Stupid. Lady thought I was trying to kill myself."

"What?"

"Yeah. She had all these weird shrink ideas. That's the last time I see a psychologist."

"What you did was awesome, Ernie. Don't let anybody tell you different." That's my Mike. He always did have a good head on him.

So it was a quiet, reflective day, just like Tim said it would be. About five o'clock, he gathered us all in the gym again.

"Okay, guys," he says. "We've all been through a lot,

and things aren't going to be exactly the same as they were before the fire. But we have eight more days of camp left, and we have to move forward. Let's all try to enjoy every day and make this last week something really special."

Mike turns and looks at me, nodding silently. More than anyone here, we both know how precious every day is.

We're heading down to dinner, the roomies and me, and it's nice to be a foursome again. We see a bunch of kids clustered in the parking lot. They're crowding around a TV news van with a telescopic satellite dish. As we approach, a boy runs up to me.

"Ernie, they're here to see you."

"Who?"

"Channel 4."

Tim, who is talking to the TV people, breaks away and comes up to me. "Ernie, local news wants to interview you about last night."

"Why?" I ask.

"Well, you're a hero, and they think it makes a great story. Look, you don't have to do this if you don't want to talk to them. I'll just get these guys to leave."

"Do it, Ernie," Mike says.

"I don't know."

Albert pulls me aside. "Dude, it's your fifteen minutes of fame. We're talking TV. Chicks watch TV! You gotta go for it." The look on his face is hard to argue with.

Seconds later, I'm standing in front of the camp sign next to Kelly Clark, the Channel 4 reporter. Kelly is pretty, but she wears way too much makeup.

Someone aims a camera at me, and a bright light is in my face. The whole camp is now gathered around, watching. The cameraman counts her into the interview.

"I'm standing in front of Camp NothinButNet, and I want you to meet a real hero. Meet fourteen-year-old Bernie Dolan."

"Ah, it's Ernie," I say sheepishly as the guys laugh.

"Ernie, so sorry. But you might want to change that to Superman. Last night, Ernie Dolan crawled into a burning building and pulled out a fellow camper, saving his life."

"Well, I had some help."

"Ernie, what made you risk your life to save that boy?"

"I don't know. But I wasn't trying to prove anything to anybody. I just went for it."

"What was going through your mind when you were in the middle of that inferno?"

"Hot. I've never felt that hot before. I was sweating like a pig."

"Maybe so, but you were cool enough to act under extreme pressure. Have you seen the boy whose life you saved?"

"Not yet."

"Well, I'm sure he's so grateful, like we all are." Kelly then turns to the campers and motions for her cameraman to follow.

"You're now looking at some of Ernie Dolan's fellow campers. Fellas, what do you think of this guy?"

Albert starts a chant, and the entire camp joins in: "Ernie! Er-nie! Er-nie!"

A chill goes right through me.

"This is Kelly Clark reporting from Camp Nothin-ButNet on the shores of Lake Michigan. Back to you, Paul."

The camera goes off, and all the guys cheer. Kelly gives me a hug and gets makeup on my shirt.

A bunch of kids gather around me as we walk into the dining hall. I fall in at the back of the line, but two guys grab me and escort me to the front.

"This is really not necessary," I say. Mike, Albert, and Derek try to crash the line too, but they're turned away. I don't feel comfortable with the special treatment, but I don't want to make a scene. I get my food and look for a table.

"Over here, Ernie."

"Sit with us."

Well, this is new. Some of these guys wouldn't have been caught dead sitting with me yesterday. I pick a table and am instantly joined by a crush of guys, who all sit around me. When my roommates walk over, there are no seats left and they have to go to another table. All I can do is shrug.

"Dolan, what was it like in there?"

"Weren't you scared?"

"Did you think Craig was dead?"

"Can't believe you're going to be on TV."

And that's how dinner goes. I answer so many questions, I can hardly eat. And although it's exhausting, I have to admit that I kind of like all the attention.

Later, in the TV lounge, a bunch of kids gather around the set to watch the local Channel 4 news. We watch the top stories of the day, then the sports and weather. Just before they sign off, the anchorman says, "And here's a great story you're not going to forget." He goes on to describe the fire and set the scene, then introduces the interview with Kelly Clark.

We all watch me on TV, and it still seems so unreal. I barely recognize myself. I look heavier and very tired, and I'm staring into the camera like a deer in the headlights. The guys all laugh when Kelly calls me Bernie. The highlight comes when the camera pans the group of campers and everyone recognizes themselves. Then the guys pick up their chant again, right there in the TV lounge.

"Er-nie! Er-nie! Er-nie!" This is starting to get a little embarrassing.

13

LIZZIE
WITH AN "L"

I'm crawling on all fours toward the shed door. Now I am inside, and the heat is unbearable. I look around for Rick Craig. He has to be in here someplace. No Craig. Then, a large part of the ceiling collapses on me, crushing my chest and pinning me to the floor. It's getting hotter and hotter as the fire closes in on me from all sides.

Now I'm burning as flames engulf me from head to toe. I close my eyes, screaming in pain. When I open them, Mike and Rick are standing nearby. Somehow, they're not on fire. They're not even sweating. They're laughing at me, actually enjoying the fact that I am burning to death. I hear their cackling laughter, louder and louder . . .

I wake up, shaking and moaning, soaked in sweat. I try to get out of bed too quickly and hit my head on the top bunk. Mike, Albert, and Derek are all out of their beds and huddled around me.

"Ernie, you okay? I think you had a nightmare," Derek says.

"It was horrible," I say. "I was burning alive . . . and Mike, you were laughing at me."

"I was? Well, I didn't mean it. It was a bad dream. It's all because of what you went through."

Tim and the other counselors talked about this. They called it post-traumatic stress. I guess it's pretty common when you go through a bad experience like we did.

The guys get me some water and a towel. I wipe my face and finally stop shaking.

Albert says, "My dreams are really strange. I had this dream once where I was really skinny and all I ate was paper clips. Then I was sucked away by a giant magnet. What do you think that means?"

"It means you're a total goofball," Mike says.

"Yeah, well, at least I don't laugh while people are burning."

⊕

As we try to make our way back to normal, the focus turns once again to the camp basketball tournament, which is really getting interesting.

Three games are left on the schedule, and they will

decide who's in the playoffs. Right now, we're tied for third place; only the top four teams will make it. And the last thing you want to do is sit around and watch everyone else play.

Mike and I are both feeling much better, and I can now take a pretty deep breath without feeling that burning sensation in my lungs. Mike has been suspended for one game for drinking, and he knows he got off lucky. Word is that Rick Craig will be getting out of the hospital today.

We're playing the Hawks, Albert's team. They're presently in fourth place, breathing right down our necks. I'm still not starting, but I'm playing more minutes than ever with Rick gone. The Hawks are led by Terry Turley, the Shaquille O'Neal of Camp NothinButNet. Turley not only leads the camp in eating, he's also the top rebounder and second leading scorer. Clearly the biggest kid in camp, he uses his size advantage to dominate the paint, getting a lot of easy baskets underneath. Turley can also hit a jump shot if left open.

To deal with Terry Turley, Coach Petrovich puts us in a zone defense designed to collapse around the big guy the second he touches the ball. This works for a while, until Turley starts passing to open teammates. If they're hitting shots, the Hawks are hard to beat.

With Craig out, Brent Sands has become our "go to"

guy, and he's risen to the occasion. Though he's increased his scoring, Brent's a point guard at heart, always looking for the pass first, trying to get all of us teammates involved. Brent's talent is his ability to throw the perfect pass at the perfect moment, hitting his man in stride for the best possible shot.

With two and a half minutes left in the game, we're down by four. Brent is bringing the ball up court. I'm being guarded by Albert Mann himself, and just like off the court, the guy never shuts up. He employs his own brand of harmless trash talk, which is pretty funny and pretty ridiculous, since Albert's the last guy who can back it up, and he knows it.

"You guys are going down, Dolan. And I'm going to shut you down personally."

"We'll see about that, Mann."

I know if I can get open, Brent will find me. I run along the baseline, stop for a split second, freezing Albert, then pop out on the wing. Sure enough, Brent hits me with a crisp bounce pass. I go up for the fourteen-foot jumper and follow the ball as it slices through the net. Now we're down by two.

"Whoops! What happened to shutting me down, Mann?" I tease Albert, who chuckles.

"Way to bust it, Ernie," Brent says as we get back on defense.

Albert gets the ball and dribbles to my area in the zone. I slide over to guard him, and out of nowhere, I run into what feels like a building. Close. It's Terry Turley, setting a screen that knocks me down hard. Albert keeps dribbling toward the basket and goes in for a layup.

"There's my highlight reel," he says. "You okay, Dolan?" Albert helps me up.

"I don't know. Are all your ribs supposed to be on the same side?"

"It helps to have King Kong on your team."

No kidding. The wind is pretty much knocked out of me, making it difficult to run the court. And each time I suck in a breath, my ribs scream in pain.

We trail by four again with just over a minute to play. I'm going on fumes now, but I've done enough bench sitting and there's no way I'm going out. One of the Hawks telegraphs a pass, and I step in front of Albert to intercept it. Brent instantly takes off for the other end, I hit him with a perfect pass, and he makes the easy layup. This brings us to within two, but the clock is not on our side. The ball goes in to Terry Turley, who backs his way toward the basket. Two other guys and I converge on him, but he powers through us like we're little girls, going in for an easy score. Turley is just too much. He takes over the final forty seconds, making two more short shots in the key, and we lose by six.

I have my best game yet: twelve points and six assists, but the loss knocks us down to fourth place. We're dangerously close to missing the playoffs, and the pressure is mounting.

⊕

The next morning, the entire camp is eating breakfast and the noise level in the dining hall is back to where it used to be, a sign that camp is returning to normal.

"Guess what," Albert says. "We're gonna meet up with the girls again today."

"How do you know?" I ask.

"Talked to Molly. She said we're having some kind of barbecue later at the lake."

"Nice," Mike says.

The news of this gets my heart jumping. Just thinking about the last time I saw these girls makes me nauseous. But this gives me another chance, and a hundred thoughts race through my head.

All of a sudden, the room goes dead silent. We look up to see Rick Craig standing at the entrance to the dining hall. A bunch of kids get up and walk over to him. As he walks farther into the room, I see that it's not really Craig, but a ghost of Craig. The swagger is gone, and he looks terrible. His hair has been shaved to a bad buzz cut, and I realize it's because most of it was burned. Several bandages cover his face, neck, and arms, and the skin that is visible is bright red. He looks like what he is: a fire victim.

The guys and I get up and join the group greeting him. Someone asks Rick if he's okay. When he answers, it's in this hoarse, raspy voice you can barely hear. It's the voice of a sick old man.

"I'm all right. It was hairy, but hey, I'm not going to let a little smoke stop me." He coughs and takes several sucking breaths from a small inhaler. "I'll be back playing soon. I'm good."

"He doesn't look good," Mike whispers.

A while later, Mike, Albert, and I are leaving the dining hall when Craig comes up to me.

"Dolan. The night of the fire . . . it's all a big blank. But I heard that somehow, you helped me out." He glances away from me to the floor. "So, whatever you did, thanks." I nod, and Craig walks away awkwardly.

"That's it?" Mike says. "That's the thanks you get for saving his life?"

"He's the same asshole he always was, just a more well-done one," Albert declares.

He's probably right, but somehow I feel sorry for

Craig. He's not used to being in a position of relying on or thanking others, and this was probably very hard for him. It was also the first time he ever spoke to me without ragging on me. Guess I'll take what I can get.

⊕

The barbecue with the girls' camp is a casual activity, with no name-tags and a lot less pressure than the dance. Although we all take showers, no one is spending too much time primping in front of a mirror.

The situation may be laid back, with less pressure, but that's for everyone else—those who didn't melt down at the dance. For me, it's still nerve-wracking, as visions of me upending the drink table flash through my head. I have to redeem myself today. I have to be able to talk to Lizzie and show her that I'm a nice, normal kid who can actually finish a sentence. I remind myself that I'm not the same geek I was a few days ago.

When we arrive at the lake around four o'clock, the girls are already there. Some are swimming, some playing volleyball, while most are soaking up the sun on towels and blankets. Tim and Laurie and several coaches are setting up the barbecues and putting out food.

The second I hit the sand, I sense a whole new vibe.

Several girls seem to be looking at me, and a couple even point. I wonder if they're talking about "that doofus" from the dance. Then, before I know it, six girls are surrounding me.

"Are you Ernie?"

I nod.

"You're the one who saved that kid in the fire."

That would be me. I cannot tell a lie. "Yes, that was me," I say as casually as possible.

"We saw you on TV."

"You're cuter in person." *Can't argue with that.*

Albert sticks his head in. "I'm his roommate who taught him everything he knows." They nudge him out of the way.

"So," one of the girls says, "what was it like being in a burning building?"

"It was bad," I say, milking it for all it's worth. "The heat was unbelievable. It melted Rick's tennis shoes. And the smoke . . . it was absolutely choking me." The girls are hanging on every word, but my roommates roll their eyes and walk away. They've heard all this before.

As cool as this is, the one girl I wish was here is lying on a towel fifty yards away. I finally break away and make my way over toward Lizzie. This time, I'm relaxed and confident. Heck, I'm Ernie Dolan, Hero. Lizzie is listening to her iPod when I walk up to her. A smile of recognition crosses her face, and she removes her ear buds. This is a good sign.

"Don't tell me," I say, pretending to remember her name. "Izzie, right?"

Luckily, she laughs. "Something like that. And you're Ernie." She sits up.

"Wow, I thought you'd permanently erase me from your memory."

"No, you were pretty hard to forget."

"I'll bet. Well, this time I can actually talk, and I promise I won't knock anything down."

She laughs. "I really felt bad for you that night."

"You did? Well, that really wasn't me, it was my evil twin who was out to get me."

"I heard about what you did."

"Oh, you mean that little fire thing?"

"Yeah, 'that little fire thing.' That was, like, the bravest thing ever."

"You think so? You know what's weird? It still feels like it all happened to someone else. All this attention, all this hero stuff—it's very strange. I mean, I'm a very average guy."

"Are you always this modest?" she asks.

"Yes. I've had a lot of practice."

Lizzie and I talk for over twenty minutes, and not another word about the fire. I find out she's from Chicago too, about a half hour from where I live.

"I can't believe we live like, three towns apart," she says. I ask all about her and find out she's fifteen, has three brothers, and plays basketball, soccer, and tennis. She wants to be a pediatrician. She's smart, funny, and real easy to talk to, not to mention totally hot.

"You want to play volleyball?" she asks.

"That depends. You're not on the volleyball team too, are you?"

"Not yet."

We join one of the volleyball games, going on the same team. Lizzie is first to serve and smashes an over-head serve that lands for an ace. She's graceful and even prettier when she's in motion.

We rotate together to the net, where Lizzie sets me up and I hit a winner. Since I don't play volleyball, I have no idea how I did that.

"Nice shot, Ernie." This girl seems to bring out the best in me.

After the game, we dive into the lake to cool off and Lizzie screams about how cold it is. We swim over to one of the docks and lie in the sun for a while, neither of us saying a word. I can't believe how comfortable I am with her. It's like, "Is this really a girl?" One glance over at her confirms that it certainly is. The combination of Lizzie's perfume and sunscreen is a scent I'll never forget. I'm lying here, thinking that this is the picture they should put on the camp brochure.

A while later, we take a canoe and paddle around the lake. Without any warning, Lizzie leans over the side and splashes me. I splash her back, and a big-time water fight is on. We both end up falling overboard into the water, laughing like crazy. Lizzie puts her arms around me and holds on tight. I can stay like this forever, but finally hoist myself into the canoe and then help Lizzie up.

Dinner is delicious as we scarf down hamburgers, hot dogs, and watermelon. As the sun slowly does its disappearing act into the water, Lizzie and I join some other kids on the dock. I introduce her to Mike, who is with a girl named Susan. Albert and Molly also join us. I'm finally one of the guys who's with a girl, and it's a great feeling to be part of this new "normal." Mike doesn't say a word to me, but there's a look on his face I know pretty well. It's a look that says, "Nice, Ernie." A look that says how happy he is for me. A look that can only come from a best friend.

It's dark, and I've never seen so many stars. We're sitting by a roaring fire alongside the lake. A few counselors and campers are playing songs on guitars. Lizzie and I are holding hands, and she puts her head on my shoulder. As I watch a star shoot across the summer sky, I realize that I'm about as happy as I've ever been.

14

THE NEW ME

It's our last game before the playoffs. We're playing the Rockets, the team we're tied with for fourth place. The winner moves on to the final four to play for the camp championship. As our team warms up, the normal joking and laughing has given way to a certain pre-game tension that's never been there before. Part of it is the pressure of knowing that we have to win to keep on playing. The other factor is the presence of Rick Craig, who hasn't been cleared to play and who now can be only a spectator.

With most of the bandages off, Craig looks a little better, but his skin is still bright red and he has a hollow, dazed appearance. Rick joins us as we shoot around, making a few shots. We start our layup line, and he stays on the court, trying to test his stamina. While we're not working at full speed, we're still moving quickly and not stopping. Rick tries to dribble in for his first layup, but before he reaches the basket, he doubles over, coughing violently. Coach P. brings out his inhaler, and Rick takes a few quick hits, finally getting some air into his lungs.

"Dat's why doctors say you can't play, Reeek," Coach says. "You just not ready yet."

Rick looks completely frustrated. The guy thinks of himself as Superman, and when he realizes that he's not, it's a harsh jolt of reality. Rick makes his way over to the bench and kicks a Gatorade jug in disgust.

As if things aren't tough enough for us, our second leading scorer, Tom Finch, is out with a sprained ankle.

Coach Petrovich pulls me aside and puts an arm around my shoulder.

"Eeernie, how you feel? You breed with your lungs?"

"Yeah, why?"

"Because you starting today."

"I am?"

"Yes. Make me pride."

"You mean proud."

"Same teeng. Just do it!"

Wow, for the first time ever in my basketball career, I'm starting. I'm pumped, even though my ribs are still sore from getting clocked with that Terry Turley pick. It only hurts when I move, but there's no way I'm going to sit.

Coach Petrovich calls the team into a huddle before the game. All the guys converge around him, except for Craig, who remains on the bench, sulking.

"Okay, guys, deez eez it. I know we been tru a lot and we down a couple guys, but play hard and smart, and you can win deez game. And if we win, we in. So let's all hang togedder and soak it up!" The guys all laugh, and Coach looks puzzled.

"The expression is '*Suck* it up,' Coach," I say.

"No time for English lesson. Just do it." Actually, his English has been improving, thanks to TV commercials. Yesterday he learned his new favorite phrase: "acid reflux."

We all put our hands in the center and yell "Kings!"

With energy and enthusiasm, we run circles around the Rockets in the first few minutes with a wicked fast break that puts them back on their heels.

I'm playing better than ever. Everything that's happened has had one big impact: my confidence level has skyrocketed. I'm taking shots I used to pass up and going for steals I never even thought about before. On defense, I'm more aggressive, staying closer to my man and contesting every shot. Okay, I'm not going to the NBA any time soon, but I feel like I'm kicking my game up to a whole other level.

The Rockets miss a jump shot, and Brent Sands goes high for the rebound. While he's still in the air, I sprint at full speed for the other end. Brent turns and rifles a baseball pass over three defenders. I catch the ball in midstride and go in for an easy layup. Textbook basketball. My side is killing me from all the running, but this is so much fun, I just "soak it up" and run harder. Hustle is contagious, as we dive for loose balls and intercept stray passes. We lead by four at halftime. I've got ten points and six assists, and it seems like I'm in every play.

The fast pace we've set starts to take its toll in the third quarter. At one point, my man beats me down court as I struggle to catch him. Time-outs are spent with our hands on our knees, trying to get our wind back. After Brent Sands is called for charging, the Rockets score again and we're now down by five points and in danger of losing.

We get a second wind midway through the fourth quarter. I hit a jump shot, and Brent hits a tough three-pointer with a guy right in his face. Brent and I are quickly learning how to play together, working off each other like we've been teammates for years.

Two minutes to play. We've cut their lead to three. Brent is carrying us down the stretch, making our last four baskets. Coach calls a time-out to give us a breather. All the guys are up from the bench, clapping and patting us on the back. All but one. Craig sits alone and kind of mimes like he's clapping. It's clearly killing him that we're doing well without his help. Albert was right about him—once an A-hole, always an A-hole.

"Okay, guys, deez eez it. You play gooood ball so far, but now we have to deeeeg deeper. I know you tired, but other team more tired dan you. Next rebound you get, try to fast break 'em. Keep on running. Now, who vants it more?"

"We vant it more!" we all yell in unison. This brings a big smile to Coach's face. We break the huddle and return to the court, wanting to win this for him as much as for ourselves.

Coach P. was right about them being tired. The Rockets miss their next shot, and I get the rebound. Brent sprints for the other end, and I lead him with a nice pass for two easy points.

"Dat's what I talkin' about!" Coach yells.

Now we're down by just a point with one minute and thirty seconds to play. We need a defensive stop. On orders from their coach, the Rockets go into a stall. With no shot clock, they can just hold the ball and run out the time. We play tough defense and try to get a steal, but they've obviously been practicing this. Three of their guys play keep-away from us by lobbing the ball over our heads. Time is running out, and with twenty seconds left, Coach Petrovich tells us to foul.

We foul Mark Stone, a pretty good shooter. Stone steps to the line and calmly drains the first free throw. We're now down by two. Stone hits the back of the rim on the next one, then Alex Crane boxes his man out beautifully, grabs the rebound, and we head down court.

Coach yells from the bench: "One goood shot!" Sixteen seconds to play. We try to get the ball to Brent, but he's being smothered by his man and another guy. Alex has the ball with ten seconds left, and he doesn't want anything to do with the last shot. As two defenders trap him in the corner, he panics and forces a weak pass. As one of the Rockets goes up to grab it, Brent smartly tips the ball away, but it's going out of bounds. With calves burning from fatigue, I sprint over and leap into the air, higher than I've ever jumped before. Everything now seems to go in slow motion. Extending my hand as far as I can, I get just enough of the ball to tap it back in bounds to Brent.

Six seconds left. Brent coolly takes two dribbles and releases a shot from just beyond the three-point line. What's the name of this camp again? Nothin' but net! We're in the playoffs.

It's my best game yet: sixteen points, seven assists,

and one memorable save. After all the high-fiving, Brent comes up to me. "That was an amazing play, Ernie. You saved the game." Coach Petrovich gathers the team around him, smiling from here to Moscow.

"You guys play great game. But too hard for me to watch. Geeves me terrible acid reflux."

I'm so grateful he didn't see a diarrhea commercial.

⊕

That night, Mike and I walk into the rec room and several guys acknowledge me, slapping my hand. Terry Turley comes up to me, handing me a ping-pong paddle. "Come on, Dolan, we're playing doubles—you and me." Two other kids actually protest, saying they want to be my partner. Rick Craig is by himself in the corner and can't believe what he's seeing.

"Whoa. When did Dolan become Mr. Popular?"

"When he saved your life, you jerk," Albert says.

That pretty much stops the room. Rick looks totally confused and embarrassed as he turns and walks out. We've heard through the grapevine that he's seeing a psychologist, but he never really talks about the fire. It's like he's pretending it never happened.

After an awkward few seconds, the room springs back

to life and I have to decide who my ping-pong partner will be. I see Mike kind of fade into the background. It's a place I know all too well.

"Tell you what, guys. Mike and I will take on anybody." Mike smiles and gets up. We play together seamlessly, beating three teams and holding the table for almost an hour. We finally take a break and sit down.

"That was fun, E. Thanks for picking me," Mike says.

"Hey, who else am I going to pick?"

"Dude, you could've picked anyone you wanted. They all want to play with you."

This kind of stops me cold as I let what Mike said sink in. For the first time ever in our friendship, I'm the more popular one. This must be as strange for him as it is for me.

A while later, we're all watching a late baseball game from the West Coast. One of the guys mutes the sound and hands me a banana. I'm pretty tired, but my audience is all looking at me, practically begging me to announce.

"Yankees one, A's nothing as we head to the bottom of the sixth. Derek Jeter steps to the plate to lead it off. Jeter takes a fastball outside, ball one."

Dead silence. This is a different game, where the action isn't so constant. I realize that this dead time has to be filled somehow.

"Jeter's looking cooler than ever in those Yankee pin-

stripes. Heck, that uniform would make Terry Turley look slim."

The guys all laugh, no one louder than Turley himself.

"Pitch to Jeter is slapped into the gap in left center. This one's going to roll to the wall, and Jeter is on his horse, rounding second and heading for third. Here comes the relay, and Jeter is . . . OUT at third! Jeter does not like the call and is face to face with Umpire Greg David-son. Jeter is giving him a piece of his mind, folks, and if I tell you what he's really saying, we'll be off the air!"

The guys crack up around me. As much fun as I'm having, I realize just how hard this announcing thing is. Every sport is different, with a different pace and rhythm. This is a skill that's going to take a lot of practice and ded-ication. As much as I like doing it and think that maybe I'd like to stick with it as a career, deep down, I wonder if I have what it takes.

It's eleven-thirty, and everyone heads for their cabins. On the way out, I see Tim, who's been working on a light fixture. I tell Mike to go on ahead, and Tim and I are all alone.

"So, how are things going?" he says.

"Pretty good."

"I'd say so. Looks like someone I know has become 'The Man.' What's it like?"

"What do you mean?"

"Well, since I've never been 'The Man,' I'm just wondering what it feels like."

What *does* it feel like? I'm not sure. It's not like I've had a lot of time in my new skin. "Well, I've got to admit, it's pretty cool . . . mostly."

"Mostly?"

"Yeah, you know, there's a downside."

"Like what?"

"Well, being the center of attention, it's . . . a little weird. Everyone's looking at you, hanging on your next word, letting you cut in line for dinner. Plus, now a lot of guys want to hang with me and I don't want to hurt anyone's feelings or leave anybody out. I'm *so* not used to this."

"So it's not easy being king."

"I'm no king. But hey, it does have its advantages. It's fun being popular. A lot more fun than how things were three days ago. The funny thing is, I'm still the same guy I was three days ago. Nothing's really changed."

Tim corrects me: "*Everything* has changed."

When I think about it, I see that Tim's right, as usual. "Well, I'm going to enjoy it while I can, because when I get back to school, I'll be the same geek looking in from the outside," I say.

Tim laughs. "I have a hunch those days are over, Dolan."

We sit there in silence for a few seconds.

"I never said thank-you," I say.

"For what?"

"You know, for what you did. For having confidence in me. For helping me believe in myself. If you ask me, *you're* 'The Man.'"

"Nah. I'm just the man behind 'The Man.'"

I laugh. Tim holds out an open palm, and I slap it.

15

LOOKING BACK AND MOVING FORWARD

It's after midnight, and Derek, Mike, and I are getting ready for bed. Albert bursts into the cabin, very excited and out of breath.

"Guys, you won't believe what I've got."

"If it's another snake, you're out of here," Mike says.

"Do you know that kid on the Hawks, Jason Fisher?"

"Skinny guy, blond hair?"

"Yes. Well, I'm hanging out in his cabin, and we're talking about the fire. Jason was there. And he just happens to mention that while he was there, he whipped out his cell phone and took a video of the whole thing."

"No way," Derek says.

"Big way. He let me see it, and it's amazing." Albert opens his right hand, revealing a high-end cell phone. "Ernie, my man, I can post this video up on YouTube, and you'll be world famous."

"Don't, Albert. No YouTube. I'm famous enough right now."

"Let's see it," Mike says.

"I will, but it's too hard for everyone to watch on a phone. Let's go down to the camp office, and I'll upload it to a laptop."

"Great idea," Derek says.

"I don't know, Albert," I say. "We're not supposed to be in there after hours."

"No one will know. We'll be in and out in ten minutes. You're gonna love this."

The guys start out, but I hesitate. Mike turns back to me. "You okay, E? Maybe you don't want to see it." They all turn and look at me.

Quite honestly, I'm not sure I do. Part of me is very curious; part of me is a little scared. I've just had my first couple of days where I didn't constantly think about the fire, and I'm not sure I want to revisit it. But good old Albert can be pretty persuasive.

"Ernie, you've got to see it. Think of this as a movie, and you're the star."

I want to tell him that this was no movie—it was very real. It was the most real day of my life. Then I realize that's exactly why I *should* see it.

The four of us quietly make our way down to the

camp office, and I'm getting more nervous by the minute. At the office, we meet Jason Fisher and two of his friends. That's more of an audience than I wanted, and I look at Albert with disapproval.

"Jason wanted to bring a couple of friends. Hey, it's his phone, his video."

We all follow Albert into the camp office. Albert and Jason make their way to a laptop computer and turn on a desk lamp. Jason fires up the computer and quickly hooks up a cable between the computer and his cell phone. Before we know it, the video appears on the seventeen-inch screen.

As everyone huddles in closer to watch, three more kids come into the office. Looks like the word has gotten out. One of the kids is Rick Craig. Jason pauses the video.

"It's the fire, Craig. Are you sure you want to see this?" Jason asks.

"Yeah, I'm sure. Just run it, okay?"

If there was tension in the room before, it's just been upped tenfold. The images on the screen are grainy, jumpy, and dark, but they do capture what happened. The first thing we see is several people running, obviously taken from the moment Jason arrived on the scene. The sound is muffled, but you can hear voices and pretty much make out what they say. The next image is like a hard slap in the face: it's the burning shed. The flames are a bright orange on the screen, and they light up the whole area. The bright light from the fire actually improves the picture quality, making things clearer. The next thing we see is Mike crawling out of the shed and me running over to him. My heart's starting to race. I steal a quick look at Mike, and he's mesmerized. You can hear a little of our conversation, followed by other voices.

"Call 9-1-1."

"Is there anyone else in the shed?"

The camera jerks around for a few seconds, taking in as much as it can. It's weird, but the rawness of the video—the grainy picture, the jerky motion—makes it seem so real. Everything went by so fast that night, it all seems like a dream. But the video is proof that it actually happened.

The next shot is of me as I crawl inside the shed, followed by a few of the coaches, who fail to stop me. There's an amazing shot of Coach Petrovich holding his hands over his eyes in horror. As I watch myself go into that shed, I realize I'm sweating right through my shirt. It's like I'm back in there all over again. For the first time, I get a real sense of how dangerous it was. I can't believe I did this.

I look to my left, and Craig is now right next to me.

He's edged his way right in front of the screen and is staring at it like he's hypnotized. We all watch in silence as my feet appear at the shed door. We see the coaches pulling me by the legs, then see me emerge. Now we see Craig being pulled out by four men, two at his arms, two at his legs. Jason's camera stays with Craig as his lifeless, unconscious body is laid on the grass. This kid captured it like a professional cameraman. Now the camera jerks around to pick up the horror on the faces of kids and coaches alike.

Back to Craig on the ground, and Laurie trying to give him CPR. The silence in the room is broken by the sound of sobbing. It's Craig, riveted to the screen as he watches what appears to be him dying. He had no memory of any of this, and the reality of it is overwhelming. Craig is now crying uncontrollably, and someone puts a hand on his shoulder. I, like everyone else in the room, don't know what to say or do. All of a sudden, Tim walks into the office.

"What the hell's going on in here?"

Several of the kids run out the door, leaving Craig, me, Mike, and Albert.

"Someone took video of the fire," Mike tells Tim softly.

Tim walks over to the screen and sees Craig crying. He watches the last thirty seconds or so along with the rest of us. The video ends, and the screen goes blank. Craig sits there like a stone, still staring at the screen and still crying. Tim comes up to him, leans over, and gives him a hug. Craig hangs on tight to Tim and cries harder.

"It's all right, Rick. Let it out."

This is quite a sight: the confident, cocky boy with the permanent swagger, always at the top of his game, reduced to a sobbing, vulnerable little kid. Rick Craig has never been more human.

Rick breaks away from Tim, wipes his eyes on his T-shirt, and tries to compose himself. He turns and faces me.

"Dolan. I didn't know. I . . . don't . . . I don't remember anything from that night. I had no idea that you . . . what you did. You saved my life, man." He's crying again.

"It's okay, Rick," I tell him.

"No. No, it's *not* okay. I was horrible to you. I treated you like crap."

"You sure did," Albert says.

"Yeah, and I hated you for it," I tell him.

"I don't blame you. I was . . . "

"A real asshole," Albert says.

"You were," Mike adds. Rick nods, acknowledging this.

"This is good, guys," Tim says nervously. "It helps to get this off your chests and clear the air."

He's right. It does feel good, so I keep going, turning

to Mike. "And you, my best friend. You turned your back on me to hang with him."

"I know. I'm sorry. But you're the one who threw a punch at me."

"You deserved it."

"Did not."

Albert jumps in. "You see what I have to live with here?" This breaks the tension. We all laugh, and even Rick flashes a little smile. The room is silent for a few seconds as we all kind of catch our collective breath. Rick walks up to me.

"Dolan. Ernie. After everything I did to you, why did you do it? Why'd you save me?"

"I don't know. I guess it was just something I had to do." Rick holds back more tears.

"I don't know what to say. Except . . . thank you."

Rick embraces me with a big hug. Over his shoulder, I see Tim look at me and wink. There's an awkward silence.

"Is this where we all sing 'Kum Ba Yah'?" Albert asks. We all crack up, and it's the best laugh I've had all week.

⊕

The camp playoffs start the next day. There are four teams left out of eight. We'll play one semifinal game, and if we win, we move on to the camp championship game. This is big, much bigger than I ever thought it would be. The whole atmosphere is ramped up. The other games were kind of casual, but now there's really something at stake. Everyone in camp watches these games, and two coaches videotape every second. They've even added a third referee, just like in the NBA.

I've never really been in a situation like this. I've never won a championship, not even in Little League. Heck, I've never even won a spelling bee. We're playing the Lakers, the second-place team. Rick Craig is getting stronger and looking better, but he's still not ready to play. He's a whole different kid now, totally into the team, slapping us on the back, giving us words of encouragement.

I'm starting again, and ten minutes before the game, Coach Petrovich comes up to me.

"Eeernie, my man. How you feel today?"

"Excited. A little nervous, but I'm ready."

"Nervous is normal. When I played, always had moths in my stomach."

"You mean butterflies."

"It was someteeng with wings. Look, you play real goood lately, so just try to keep up dat."

"I'm not going to let you down, Coach."

I've never started in a big game before, but I've been gaining confidence with every game, and I'm beginning to hit my stride. I'm actually looking forward to the pressure. The horn sounds to end the warm-up period, and Coach gathers us in a huddle.

"Okay, fellas. Rebound, defend, take care of ball, and play togedder. Oh, and have much fun."

"Guys." Rick addresses the huddle. "The doctor says if I pass a breathing test, I can play tomorrow. You win this one, and I'm passing that test. Now, go kick some butt."

This really pumps us up. The Lakers are a very good team with talented guys at several positions. Their best player is Sammy Moore, a six-foot forward who can do it all. In his last game, Moore scored thirty points, a camp high.

The first few minutes of the game are very sloppy, with both teams feeling the extra tension. Turnovers, traveling calls, missed shots—I wouldn't want to be watching this so far. Both teams settle down after the first quarter, and the game changes for the better.

Tom Finch, our power forward, is back after his sprained ankle. Tom really sets the pace in the second quarter, gobbling up rebounds and starting fast breaks. I'm the recipient on one of those breaks, and my first basket gets me going. Brent Sands is the coolest one out there, directing the team like a real point guard. He's paying special attention to me, feeding me with crisp, accurate passes. I hit two jump shots in a row, and after the second one, I hear the strangest thing: "Great shot, Ernie!" It's Rick cheering me from the bench, something I never thought I'd hear.

Sammy Moore plays like the star he is, driving in for layups and hitting shots from all over the floor. Halfway through the fourth quarter, the Lakers lead us 49-41. Brent gets hot, hitting three shots in a row, and we're now down by two. The pace is incredibly fast, and I'm gasping for air. Coach calls a time-out to give us a rest and set up a play.

"Okay, boys, sit down, catch breaths."

"Excuse me, Coach," Rick says. "I've been noticing something. Ernie's man is starting to cheat every time Brent drives the lane." He's right. Brent's been so hot, my defender has started to leave me and go to him. "Have Brent penetrate, then kick it to Ernie."

"Okay," Coach says. "You guys cleeer out and let Brent go one-on-one. Eeernie, the second your man leave you, break for basket."

How cool is this? I've never had a play called especially for me before, and I get one in a playoff game, thanks to Rick. It feels great. As we go back on the court, I suck in as much air as I can.

Alex Crane inbounds the ball to Brent, and the four of us clear out to the right of the key. The Lakers already look confused. Brent is now isolated with his man on the left side. He dribbles around for a few seconds, crosses him over, then heads for the basket. Sure enough, my defender is the first guy to meet him. I cut for the hole, and my shoes squeak loudly across the hardwood. Brent lobs a perfect pass that lands softly in my hands. I lay it up and in off the glass, just like we planned it. Coach P. and Rick lead the cheers from the bench, and I point to Rick as a gesture of thanks.

The lead goes back and forth until Sammy Moore fouls out with two minutes to play. Brent makes some key shots, and the Lakers never recover. We pull away for a six-point victory. The guys from the bench run out onto the floor, led by Rick.

"Great game, Ernie," he says, giving me five. Coach P. goes around hugging each one of us.

"You guys were awesome. Deez eez proudest I've been since I learned to speak English!"

"You speak English?" Brent asks.

The win puts us into the camp championship game

against the Pacers and their best player—and my best friend—Mike. Now it *really* gets interesting.

16

CRUNCH TIME

The championship game is at two o'clock, and the entire camp is buzzing about it. Kids are making bets and running pools for the final score. After a light lunch around noon, I head back to the cabin to get into my uniform. I find Mike there, getting dressed.

"Hey, Mike."

"Hey. So, this is it. One game for all the marbles."

"Winner take all," I add.

"A lot of pressure. You ready for that?"

I laugh at this. It's the same old Mike who would try to psych me out in our driveway games.

"Nice try, Mike. Didn't work then, ain't gonna work now. I'm totally ready."

"Good. Me too. You guys going with a zone defense?" Mike asks.

"Like I'm going to tell you," I shoot back.

Mike laces up his shoes and grabs his gym bag. "Good luck, E."

"You too, man." We slap hands, and he heads out. I sit on my bed and close my eyes, trying to relax. Ten seconds later, my cell rings. It's Lizzie.

"Hey you."

"Lizzie, hi! What's up?"

"Just want to say good luck today."

"Thanks."

"I'll be there watching and cheering you on."

"That's great. I feel like I've won already."

"Not so fast, hotshot. I'm no basketball expert, but I think you have to play the game first."

"Thanks for clearing that up," I say.

"I'd say 'break a leg,' but I think that's for actors."

"Yeah, you *definitely* don't want to say that to a basketball player."

"Okay, well, you get the idea. Have a great game, Ernie."

"I will, now. Thanks a lot for calling."

I hang up, totally pumped. I thought I was ready before, but now I'm *really* ready.

⊕

"Welcome to the thirtieth annual Camp NothinBut-Net championship game." Tim stands at center court in front of a packed gym. Every seat is filled with our entire camp, plus the whole girls' camp. People are standing two deep along the baseline. I'm telling you, this is crazy.

Tim points to the Wall of Champions, decorated with the names of players from every winning team. Then he names the prizes the winners will receive: an NBA jersey with our name, video games, and, finally, the big prize—a free two-week session next summer at Camp Nothin-ButNet.

If the first playoff game was big, this can only be described as huge. Just like in an NBA game, each team is introduced, player by player. They announce my name, and as I run out to slap hands with my teammates, the chant begins.

"Er-nie! Er-nie! Er-nie!" The gym is rocking. What an amazing feeling. First, I'm embarrassed, and then really touched. The hairs on the back of my neck stand up, my throat gets tight, and I have to bite my lower lip to stop it from trembling.

As we go over to our bench to huddle up, I quickly scan the crowd. Lizzie is in the fourth row behind our bench. She gives me the thumbs-up sign, and I nod back. Tim and Laurie watch from the first row at center court.

We gather on the sideline, and I see that every guy on our team has already broken out in a sweat. Coach Petrovich brings us all together in a circle. "Guys, no matter what happen, I proud of each and only one of you." We all laugh at this, and it loosens us up. "What I say this time? Okay, deez eeez the big one. We a real goood team now, and eef we play like team, we can win da whole burrito."

"Enchilada," Brent says politely.

"Dat too," Coach comes back, grinning.

We all put our hands in the middle and shout "Win!"

This game is a contest between two very even teams. The Pacers finished in first place, winning two more games than we did. They're led by Mike, who's been playing the best basketball of his life. They also have our roommate, Derek Singleton, an excellent player at both ends of the court, and Jamal King, a very good point guard who matches up well against our Brent Sands. We've played these guys twice and split the two games. Of course, that was with Rick Craig playing full games. Today he's been cleared to play, but only for ten minutes, so he's not starting. I walk over to Rick on the bench as he's taking a hit on his inhaler.

"You okay?" I ask.

"Fine. These guys are fast, Ernie, so make sure you get back on defense." I nod, and we slap hands.

As we get ready for the opening tip, my heart starts pounding. This is the biggest game of my life, and I really want to play well. People I care about are watching, and my coach and teammates are depending on me. But more important, I need this one for me. I have to prove to myself that I can play well under intense pressure when it really counts.

All of a sudden, the crowd starts in again: "Er-nie! Er-nie! Er-nie!" Gee, no pressure there.

The game starts at a blistering pace. Both teams are pushing the ball after every missed shot, and the fast breaks result in a lot of quick layups. The crowd is screaming and stomping, which makes it all the more exciting.

Without Rick to guard Mike, the assignment goes to Tom Finch. Tom is a little taller than Mike, but definitely not as quick. Mike blows by him several times for easy baskets, and before we know it, we're down by seven. Coach calls a time-out and tells us to go into our zone defense. This way, whenever Mike has the ball, he'll draw the attention of two or three players. Rick now goes into the game for the first time.

It's a little strange being on the same court with him again. After a couple of minutes, it's clear that Rick is not the same player he was before the fire. He still has all the skills, but not much stamina, and it's hard for him to get into a rhythm. But the thing that's really missing is that confidence. He's very tentative for the first few possessions and almost looks afraid.

Life is so strange. The fire and its aftermath changed everyone in some way. It gave me a big shot of confidence, while Rick's is going in the other direction. Still, Rick at fifty percent is better than almost everyone in camp. Realizing he's compromised now, he becomes a real team player, passing, screening, and doing the little things that help win games. After missing his first two shots, Rick makes two in a row, and Mike says, playfully, "He's back."

We're down by three when Rick grabs a rebound and clears it out to me on the wing. I spot Brent up court and try to snap him a pass, but there's very little snap and Derek intercepts it. Then he deftly hits Mike with a bounce pass, and Mike converts the layup. Not exactly my best moment, but I'm not discouraged. I'm quickly learning that in this game, just like in life, there's always another play. I tell myself to calm down.

A minute later, I come off a screen and Brent hits me with a nice pass. This time, I'm more relaxed, and I can feel the shot going in the second it leaves my hand. *Is it my imagination, or is the crowd cheering louder for me?*

I run back to play defense, and Rick is the first one to slap my hand.

"Way to bust it, Ernie."

Midway through the second quarter, we're trailing by four. Brent sets a screen for me, then rolls to the basket. I hit him with a bounce pass, and he goes in for an uncontested score. As we run back on defense, he points at me, acknowledging the good play we both made.

Jamal is bringing the ball up the court for the Pacers. As Brent hounds him, Tom Finch also comes over and traps him in the corner. Jamal gets rattled, and I'm right there when he throws the errant pass. Rick instinctively takes off for the other end, and I rifle a perfect baseball pass into his hands. Two more points for us.

The Pacers miss their next shot, and I join Brent and Rick on a fast break. Rick drives the lane, draws two defenders, flips a no-look pass back to me, and I make the layup. We're now up by two, and the Pacers call time out.

The crowd is going crazy, stomping so hard I'm afraid they're going to collapse the stands. It's become pretty clear that the majority of fans here are rooting for us. Every time I score, they chant my name again.

On the sideline, we all exchange high fives. Rick takes a seat on the bench and sucks on his inhaler. He gave it everything he had for four minutes and he's exhausted, but it gave us an emotional lift. You can see the determination in everyone's eyes. In our last game, we finally have turned into a real team.

That one-minute stretch is what basketball is all about: five guys playing as one. Everyone in perfect synch, doing his part. When this happens—and it doesn't happen very often—basketball becomes a simple and beautiful game. There is nothing else like it.

We take a six-point lead at the half. In the third quarter, the battle intensifies. The play is becoming more and more physical, with anyone going in for a layup getting hammered.

With Rick still resting on the bench, the Pacers go on a nice run, as Jamal King and Mike each hit a couple of three-pointers. Brent and I answer with jumpers of our own, but as the quarter ends, we find ourselves down by three.

As the teams take the floor for the fourth quarter, the crowd gives us a rousing standing ovation. My body's aching from all the contact, and I take a few deep breaths, trying to get my wind back. There's a pretty good reason I'm tired: for the first time ever, I've played every minute of the game.

The game is living up to its hype, as the lead changes constantly. We go on a spurt, they go on a spurt. Mike is playing out of his mind, and despite gasping for breath on almost every play, Rick is playing his heart out, which makes all of us want to do the same.

Tom Finch grabs a rebound and fires a quick outlet pass to Brent as I sprint down court. I go in for what I think is an easy layup, but Mike, coming out of nowhere, swats the ball into the second row. He smiles at me, and I smile back, giving him props for a good play. It's the play of the game so far, pumping up the Pacers and the crowd. The Pacers go on a short run and take a 42-38 lead with six minutes left in the game.

I steal a Jamal King pass and feed Tom Finch for two points. Mike is hitting shots from all over the floor, and Rick's competitive nature propels him to hit some tough shots of his own to keep us in the game. But I can see that Rick is starting to lose steam, especially at the defensive end. Mike goes right by him for an easy layup, and the Pacers lead 49-48 with three minutes and twenty-five seconds left to play.

Coach P. calls time out, and Rick comes out, saying he's through for the day. He gave it everything he had, and the crowd gives him a standing ovation.

"You boys playing gooood. Remember, pressure dem on defense and stay aggressive on offense."

We try to hang in there without Rick. On offense, we

pound the ball in to Tom Finch. The Pacers foul Tom, who's not a great free-throw shooter. Tom misses both free throws, and the Pacers bring the ball down. I'm guarding Derek, who is definitely not an easy cover. He fakes me one way, then cuts under the basket—the old backdoor play. Mike hits him with the pass, and Derek scores. A minute and twenty seconds to play, and now we're down by three.

Brent hits a jumper from the wing, cutting the Pacers' lead to 53-52. We still play our zone, but it makes no difference to Mike. He gets a screen at the top of the key and puts up a perfect arching shot that slices through the net.

"Mike, take it easy on us, will you?" I beg.

"Not a chance, E."

We're losing 55-52 with a minute left to play. Mike has twenty-four points, a bunch of big rebounds, and is clearly the best player on the court. This, of course, makes me want to beat him that much more.

Tom deflects a pass into my hand, and Brent and I take off on a two-on-one fast break. I feed Brent for the layup, and we're back within one, 55-54. The crowd has been on its feet the entire quarter and is now screaming with every play, pumping us up even more, if that's possible.

Twenty-nine seconds left. It doesn't get any closer

than this.   It's the ultimate pressure situation, yet, strangely, I'm not feeling a whole lot of pressure. The old me would've wilted by now. I tell myself, as big as this game is, it's still just a game. Hey, I've been in a burning building. Now, *that's* pressure. A basketball game is nothing compared to a real life-or-death situation.

With this in mind, a peaceful kind of calm comes over me. I quickly take it all in: the crowd, the court, the players. This is the most fun I've ever had playing, and I'm going to enjoy every last second of it.

The Pacers want to protect their one-point lead and start running the clock down. Twenty-five seconds. Twenty-one seconds. Jamal and Mike are the only ones touching the ball, but they're such great dribblers, it's impossible to get to them.

Eleven seconds. Mike has the ball. "Foul heem!" Coach P. yells from the bench. This is definitely the right strategy, as we have to get the ball back to have any chance. But Mike has been in the zone, that magical place where you feel you just can't miss. If we foul him, he'll most likely make the two free throws and we'll have to hit a three-point shot just to tie.

Tom Finch runs over to foul Mike, but gets caught in a screen. Nine seconds. Mike's coming my way. It's me and him, just like in the driveway all these years. I've watched Mike so often, I know all of his moves. There's one move that I have a special place for in my memory bank. I know for a fact that when he crosses over from left to right, Mike always tips it off with a certain head fake.

"Foul heem!" Coach Petrovich screams again.

Six seconds. I come up as if to foul Mike, and, sure enough, there it is: the head fake. Only this time, I'm ready for it. I instantly step to my left the exact second Mike dribbles that way. I flick my hand out and swipe the ball, picking him clean. Mike is so surprised, he actually freezes for a split second. And that split second is all the time I need.

I take off like a rabbit for the other end. With one quick glance at the clock, I see three seconds left. Now my eyes are like lasers, focused on only one thing: the basket. Dribbling faster than I ever have before, I feel drops of sweat slide down my forehead into my left eye. It burns like crazy, and my eye closes instinctively.

But there's no way this is going to stop me. I'm under the right side of the backboard, just where I want to be. And then, everything goes into slow motion. I hear nothing but silence, as I have blocked out the screaming crowd. *Don't miss. Please don't miss.*

With all my adrenaline pumping, I lay the ball up a

185

bit too hard. It comes off the backboard and bounces on the rim . . . once . . . twice . . . and on the third bounce, it drops in, just as time runs out.

The next few minutes are a complete blur. Rick runs to me and lifts me into the air. My other teammates follow, and before I know it, I'm lying on the court with bodies on top of me. It's like we just won the NCAA tournament.

The crowd chants louder than ever: "Er-nie! Er-nie! Er-nie!" The guys pick me up and congratulate me, one by one.

"You won it for us, Ernie," Brent says.

"Best feenish I ever see!" Coach Petrovich screams.

"That was so totally clutch, man!" Rick yells. I laugh.

I scan the crowd for Lizzie, but I can't find her. Tim comes up to me, grinning widely and extending his hand.

"Not bad, kid. Not bad at all."

Someone taps me on the shoulder. I turn around to Lizzie's smiling face. "You were amazing." She gives me a big hug, not caring at all how sweaty I am.

In all the excitement, there's one person I'm missing. Where's Mike? As the crowd thins, I look around the gym. Mike is sitting all alone, slumped against the wall in the corner. I excuse myself from Lizzie and walk over to him.

"Great game, Ernie."

"Talk about great games, you were amazing, Mike."

"Not amazing enough. How'd you ever pick me like that?"

"I took a chance, and I got lucky."

"It wasn't luck, man. You know my game better than anyone else. No more one-on-one in the driveway." I laugh. Mike puts out his hand, and I help him up. He's exhausted and deflated, but still manages a smile when he says, "Congratulations, E."

And, for a few precious seconds, I savor the moment. I finally came through in a big game. When it counted. In the clutch, I stepped up.

17

THE LAST DAY

Hard as it is to believe, it's the last night of camp. We're in the gym for the camp awards ceremony. The mood is light and jovial, but not without a little sadness. I've met some terrific people who I'm really going to miss.

Tim Sanders announces the winners of the camp basketball championship. Our team steps down to the floor, where Tim and Coach Petrovich hand us our trophies and prizes.

The lights suddenly dim, and a spotlight hits the Wall of Champions. A banner is released with the Kings logo and each team member's name. It's a special feeling, knowing that my name will be on this wall forever. It's also not a bad feeling to know that I can come back to Camp NothinButNet for a free session next summer.

Next, Tim announces the individual awards. "The Most Valuable Player award was not an easy choice this summer. There were many excellent players who turned in memorable performances. Taking into consideration consistency, leadership, unselfishness, and overall impact on one's team, the coaches have chosen Mike Rivers as the MVP of Camp NothinButNet."

Everyone cheers, none louder than me. Mike really deserves it after carrying his team to within a point of the championship. He's a little embarrassed as he accepts the trophy, thanking his coach and teammates.

Tim steps to the podium again. "The award for the best camp prank goes to a truly inspired man, Albert Mann." Thunderous applause as Albert bounces down the stands to the court, where he does a funny little dance.

"I'd like to thank the academy," he says, wiping fake tears from his eyes. "This has been a lifelong dream of mine. I owe all of my success to my good friend, Sly." Albert takes out his fake rat from under his shirt, and the campers go wild. "Seriously though, being the court jester isn't always easy. You never know if people are laughing with you or at you. But, at least they're laughing." He hands the microphone back to Tim and receives a big round of applause.

"The Most Inspirational Camper award has been given out every year, but this year, it has a special meaning. As we all know, this session was not exactly camp as usual. We were faced with a near tragedy, and we were very fortunate that everyone survived. The recipient of this award showed amazing courage, sacrificing his safety to save a fellow camper. His inner strength, his character, and his concern for fellow campers sets an example for all of us, both on and off the court. Because of this, we are naming this award for him, and it will be known from now on as the Ernie Dolan Most Inspirational Camper Award. Let's hear it for Ernie Dolan!"

Everyone stands and applauds. As I walk down to the floor, the chant begins: "Er-nie! Er-nie! Er-nie!" A guy could get used to this.

All the coaches line up to congratulate me. Tim shakes my hand and gives me a plaque with my name engraved on it. I face my fellow campers with a mixture of pride and embarrassment.

"Wow. I don't know what to say. They're naming an award after me, and I'm not even dead yet." Everyone laughs, and I instantly feel more relaxed. There's not much else to say, but I do know that I have to thank someone, and there's no better time than now.

"There's a guy here we all know. He kind of runs this place. He blows up our basketballs, screws in our light bulbs, even tastes our ice cream. He's a counselor, a teacher, but mostly, he's a friend. He's the man who helped me see the person I could really be, and I'll never forget him for that. Thank you, Tim Sanders."

As everyone applauds, Tim walks over to me and whispers in my ear, "I won't be forgetting you any time soon either, Dolan."

⊕

Everyone's in the parking lot, waiting for our rides home, with suitcases and duffle bags scattered in every direction. Whoever said that it's hard to say good-bye didn't know the half of it. The ritual of saying good-bye is more complicated than ever, as we exchange phone numbers and addresses, e-mail addresses and MySpace sites. I've met some great people and hope we can all stay in touch, but who knows? Over time and distance, people tend to lose track of each other.

Mike and I say good-bye to our roommates. Derek turned into a very cool guy. Albert is one of a kind, and I'll always remember him reaching out to me after that disastrous pick-up game. As a parting gift, Albert gives me Sly, his fake rat. As weird as it seems, it's one of the nicest gifts I've ever received.

Laurie Sanders comes up to me and gives me a big hug. "Well, this has been an experience."

"To say the least," I say.

"You're an amazing young man, Ernie Dolan. You better keep in touch with us."

"Don't worry, I will. And thank you for everything."

Rick Craig is standing nearby with his parents. He's almost back to looking normal, except for a few red patches of skin on his arms.

"Mom, Dad, I want you to meet Ernie Dolan, the kid who saved my life."

Rick's mother hugs me so hard she almost cracks a rib. "Bless you, Ernie," she says. Rick's dad looks like he's going to cry as he shakes my hand with both of his.

"I don't know how to thank you, son."

"You're welcome, sir."

Rick pulls me off to the side for a private word.

"I don't know what to say, man. Words were never my thing. But you're the reason I'm still here."

"Yeah, well, I guess we're all good at something," I say, trying to keep it light.

Rick laughs. "You're going to be good at a lot of things. Promise me you'll come visit some time. We can ride horses, go sailing, play hoops."

"I'd like that."

Rick hugs me, we slap hands, and he takes off. As I watch him go, I think about how funny life is sometimes.

The kid who was my worst nightmare ended up changing my life.

I turn around to see Coach Petrovich walking toward me, smiling.

"Eeernie. Had to come say good-byes to you."

"I'm going to miss you, Coach."

"Eet was pleasure knowing you. You are very special boy."

"Thanks. And I can't thank you enough for teaching me the game."

"Tanks for teaching me da English."

"You're getting better every day," I say.

"You have to promise to keep touching me."

"You mean 'keep in touch,'" I say, and we both laugh.

Coach gives me a big Russian bear hug, lifting me off the ground and dropping me back down. I'm never going to forget this guy.

The crowd in the parking lot is thinning out as more kids leave. Mike's parents aren't coming for us for another hour, so I've asked Tim for a big favor. He's going to drive me to the girls' camp so I can say good-bye to Lizzie. We said good-bye on the phone last night—twice—but I really want to surprise her in person.

"You have no idea what this means to me," I yell to Tim, sitting behind him on his Harley as he maneuvers the bike around the narrow lake road and the wind whips me in the face.

"Oh, but I do. There was this woman once who I swam across a lake for."

"Yeah? What happened to her?"

"I married her. She's the hot one, remember?"

Just then a car careens around the curve, and Tim has to swerve the bike off the road. He hits the brakes just before we hit a tree.

"Moron!" he yells. Two women get out of the car and come over to us.

"Sorry," the older one says. The younger one—*is that who I think it is?*

"Ernie?"

"Lizzie?"

I get off the Harley and run over to her. "What are you doing here?"

"I wanted to surprise you before you left."

"No way! That's where I was going—to surprise you and say good-bye in person!"

Lizzie and I hug for a good few seconds and then realize Tim and the other woman are watching. I turn to them. "Can a guy have a minute?" Tim and the lady walk off down the trail, and Lizzie and I are alone.

"Promise you're going to come and see me," Lizzie says.

"As soon as I get home," I say. "I've got it all mapped out. If I take the number 3 bus, I can be at your house in thirty minutes. How cool is that?"

"Very cool. Just wait until I get home first."

"When's that?"

"Friday night."

"How about Saturday night?" I ask.

"You're on."

And there it is. My first date. Gee, this was easier than I thought. Lizzie and I just smile at each other for a few seconds. Then someone honks a horn, and we start to say good-bye. Then, she kisses me. It's a great kiss, but I make a mental note that if we ever do it again, I have to watch those braces.

As I watch her walk down the road to her car, my heart sinks a little. I walk back over to Tim.

"So?" he says.

"So what?"

"So, how did it go?"

"Fine. We said good-bye."

Tim laughs.

"What's so amusing?"

"You kissed her, didn't you?"

"Maybe. How do you know?"

"How do I know? That smile on your face is going to last a month."

Once again, he's right.

18

SEVEN YEARS LATER

It's a funny thing when you're a kid. You have days when you can't wait until you grow up and become an adult, and days when you just want to be fourteen forever. Well, take it from me, you *do* grow up, and it happens before you know it. The journey is filled with excitement, anxiety, challenges, and wonder.

I'm twenty-one now and a senior at the University of Indiana. I've lived another third of my life since I left Camp NothinButNet. That sports announcing bug that bit me at camp never left. I returned home that summer and really got into announcing. I'd turn down the volume on sporting events and practice calling the action myself. As the years went by, I did it over and over, announcing all kinds of sports, driving my parents nuts, until they finally put a TV in my bedroom so they wouldn't have to hear me.

My interest continued and grew when I started college at Indiana as a sports broadcast major. I did sports updates and talk shows, called games, and got behind the microphone every chance I could.

I had several internships with local sports stations, gaining valuable experience. My hard work paid off, as I became the school's play-by-play announcer for football and basketball games, which put me on the map in Bloomington, Indiana.

In pursuit of my dream job, I'm lucky to have the most amazing person by my side—my girlfriend, Lizzie. That's right, Lizzie from camp. We started seeing each other right after camp and never stopped. Lizzie enrolled at Indiana a year before me. She's the smartest person I know, and has already been accepted to medical school.

A while ago, I tried out for a contest held by ESPN called Dream Job. It's a televised competition between eight contestants, all wanna-be broadcasters. The winner gets a one-year contract as a sports reporter for ESPN. I submitted tapes and videos of my work and survived several grueling interviews. Now, for the big news: last week, I was chosen to be one of the contestants! I'm in New York right now for the first day of the contest, which starts in two hours. Make that an hour and fifty-five minutes.

I've been up since six A.M., taken two showers, and

brushed my teeth three times. With Lizzie's help, I bought a new blue suit for the contest, along with several shirts and three killer ties. If I'm ever going to be in front of a camera, I'm going to have to learn how to dress.

I have to be at the ESPN studio in Times Square at ten A.M. It's eight-thirty, and I'm getting in a cab for the mile ride downtown. Ninety minutes to go a mile; what could go wrong? You had to ask.

Another cab cuts off a produce truck. The produce truck careens around the corner on two wheels and turns over in the middle of 74th Street. Lettuce, tomatoes, carrots, and celery are rolling in every direction. After cursing in some strange language, my taxi driver turns to me.

"I hope you have a good book, kid, 'cause we're going to be here a while."

Great. My entire career sabotaged by a runaway salad. I pay the driver and get out of the cab, carefully stepping over and around the crushed tomatoes. I'll just walk the thirty blocks.

After three steps, I realize the new loafers I just bought do not quite fit. Every step I take is agony, as the back of my left shoe digs like crazy into my heel. Two blocks later, I take off my shoes and walk in my socks. No problem, I can do this.

Then another crazy cab driver speeds next to the curb,

right through a huge puddle. New York City's finest sewage splashes up and soaks my new pants. Not exactly the look I'm going for.

I walk faster, hoping my increased speed will dry my pants against the breeze. Well, I've always been a dreamer. But in the real world, these pants wouldn't dry if they were on the sun. I decide to go into a men's store on 57th Street. The salesman takes one look at me and starts laughing.

"Oooops! Someone had an accident."

"I don't have time to explain. Just find me some pants." He pulls out a pair that he swears goes with my jacket, and once again, I'm dressed for success. By now, it's nine forty-five and I still have to walk eleven blocks.

Nine fifty-seven. I arrive at the ESPN studios, out of breath, sweaty, and with holes on the bottom of both socks. I put my shoes back on and enter the building. I'm ushered into another room, where seven other people—my competition—are already there, all bright-eyed, not sweating, and, I'm sure, without holes in their socks.

I take a seat and catch my breath while I look over the other contestants. There are five men and two women. They all look like they could be sportscasters, but hey, so do I.

A young woman comes out with a clipboard and asks me to sign in. I get up, trying to look as cool as possible, and notice several people chuckling. Even the lady signing me in is smiling, and she seems to be looking at my butt.

"Nice pants. Do you know you still have the price tags on them?"

To my horror, I look behind me and see the tags on the back of my pants. I was in such a hurry that I ran out of the store without taking them off. Now everyone in the room is having a laugh at my expense. I think about trying to explain how this happened, but instead I just say, "Long story."

I take the tags off my pants and sit down, trying to put the best face I can on embarrassment. Not the start I was hoping for. But, as I learned in that great life lesson seven years ago at camp, how you start isn't necessarily how you finish.

Six of the eight contestants are college students who broadcast for their school. The other two actually have some professional sports experience. The competition is stiff, but I've been preparing for this for seven years, ever since the time I grabbed that first banana.

The contest is judged by a panel of three ESPN professionals—two producers and *SportsCenter* anchor John Anderson. The host is Stuart Scott, one of the longtime stars of ESPN, most known for his famous catchphrase, "Boo-ya!"

The first round of competition requires us to do play-by-play on back-to-back clips—one from baseball, one from basketball. Each clip runs for two minutes, and they've turned the broadcast sound off so we can supply our own call. No one's more prepared for this than me, thanks to my parents, who had the good sense not to throw me out of the house all those years.

I walk into the studio, and it's like nothing I've ever seen. A dozen monitors, several replay machines, tons of lights, and three state-of-the-art cameras. This really *is* the big time.

The game clips are action-packed, which makes them easier to call. I come through this phase with flying colors. Two other contestants are eliminated, and it's now down to a group of six.

The next challenge is to interview an athlete. Well, not really an athlete, but an actor playing an athlete. For my interview, I draw Roger Clemens, one of the great pitchers of all time and a guy who's played into his forties. I know a little about Clemens, but this isn't as easy as it looks, as the actor playing him tries to throw me by giving a couple of very brief non-answers. This does send me off track for a few seconds, but I dig deeper and come up with fresh new questions. I save the interview when I ask "Clemens" about his amazing dedication to training, asking specific questions that won't result in two-word answers. The judges vote, and I make the cut again. Eight contestants have now been reduced to four.

The next segment is a lot of fun, as each of us gets to sit in with ESPN's Tony Kornheiser as a co-host of his popular show, *Pardon the Interruption*. It's not easy keeping up with Tony, who is quick-witted and has a unique view of sports and their place in the world. I try to leave the funny stuff to him, but do score some points when I say that watching soccer is like watching paint dry. This was a little bit risky, but I've watched the show enough to know how Tony feels about soccer and its lack of scoring.

As the judges are about to announce the two finalists, my heart is in my throat. The first one announced is Kevin Foley, a senior at Syracuse University, and possibly the smoothest guy here. I tell myself that it's been an amazing experience and whatever happens, I know I gave it my best effort. It seems like forever until they announce the other finalist, and, believe it or not, it's me!

I'm in the finals for the Dream Job and a shot at being a professional sportscaster.

⊕

Now it's the day of the final competition. Minutes before the broadcast, I try to calm myself, thinking about the road I've taken and all I've been through to get here. Most of my thoughts go back to my life-changing experience at Camp NothinButNet. I think about the people I met there, the horrible lows and the amazing highs, and how it all helped mold me into the person I am today.

For the final competition, the judges are going to put the two of us side by side, and we'll co-anchor a mini-version of *SportsCenter*, the show that made ESPN the gold standard of sports networks.

As much as Kevin Foley is my opponent and the guy standing in my way of winning, we have to work together as a team, just like the real co-anchors of any *SportsCenter* show.

Reading a teleprompter is not a problem, since I have some experience with it, but on a show like this, a producer is always talking to you through your earpiece, cueing you and counting down the segments. It takes all my concentration to hear what he's saying without letting it distract me.

"Good evening. Welcome to *SportsCenter*. I'm Ernie Dolan, along with Kevin Foley."

We're off and running. I start with a clip about the Dallas Mavericks winning their fourteenth straight game. It goes flawlessly; so far, so good. Kevin narrates a couple of other NBA highlights, and it's back to me.

"If the Phoenix Suns sustain any more injuries, their mascot may have to suit up. We go to Phoenix, where the Suns bravely took on the Lakers." Just then, the video goes down and I'm left hanging without a picture. This is my first real test. I can't just read my script, because it's written to match the video, so I'm just going to have to wing it. "Looks like the Suns just burned out," I ad-lib. I go on to deliver a quick summary of the big plays and the final score. I survive the mini-crisis, but I can't say the same for my shirt, which is now drenched.

As Kevin narrates a hockey highlight, a voice from the control room tells him to stretch the segment for twenty seconds. He ad-libs some comments, then, out of nowhere, puts me on the spot.

"Just what do the Islanders need to do to win a game, Ernie?" I'll be damned if I know, but I'd better say something, and fast.

"Watching that clip, I'd say they need to take better advantage of their power plays." Kevin agrees with me, and we move on to the next highlight. This is the real pressure of a live broadcast—you never know what's going to happen, and you have to be ready for anything. And I love it.

We make it through the test broadcast, and although I stumbled on a couple of words, I think it went as well as could be expected. To be honest, Kevin and I were both strong and it won't be easy for the judges to pick a winner.

The judges praise our overall performance, then offer some constructive criticism, telling me that I have to slow down in general and make better transitions between segments.

As Kevin and I stand side by side on camera, waiting for them to announce the winner, I think back to all those Academy Awards shows I've watched. When they announce the winner of a major award, the cameras are on all the nominees, capturing each of their reactions. I always marvel at how the people who don't win manage to keep their cool, keep smiling, and somehow not show their disappointment. I tell myself that if I don't win, I have to be like those actors.

"And the winner of the fourth Dream Job contest is . . . Ernie Dolan!"

Somehow, I didn't exactly prepare for this. I'm elated and want to scream. I can't wait to scream, but not here, not now. Aside from the biggest smile of my life, I keep my cool. I shake Kevin Foley's hand and tell him I hope we work together again some day.

But it's almost too much to comprehend: I, Ernie Dolan, am going to be a sports reporter for ESPN!

Lizzie meets me backstage and jumps into my arms.

A half hour later, the two of us are outside in the middle of Times Square, screaming with joy. We probably look like a couple of lunatics, but this being New York, no one even notices.

19

A DREAM
COME TRUE

Eight weeks later, I start my sports broadcast career as a sideline reporter for ESPN. My first assignment is a college classic, the Michigan–Ohio State game. I'm on the field in Ann Arbor, looking around the stadium at 100,000 fans. In my wildest dreams—and I had a lot of those—I never thought it would be this exciting. I take a second and actually pinch myself just to make sure I'm not dreaming.

It's forty minutes to game time. The producer has briefed me about my assignment. I'm starting with a "grab." This is TV talk for a quick pre-game interview with the Ohio State coach.

During the game, I will cruise both sidelines, getting information on player injuries and anything else that might be relevant. I'm told they will go to me for a live report two times in each half.

My mouth is dry and I'm nervous, but it's the good kind of nervous. I've done my homework, memorizing every player by number and studying a fifty-page research packet of vital information and some meaningless trivia. I'm probably the only one on the planet who knows that the Michigan punter has six toes on his right foot.

Another reason I'm feeling good is that I have a very special fan club here with me today. Along with Lizzie, my mom and dad are here, along with Mike, still my best friend in the world.

I also invited a special group of friends—the ones I met seven years ago at Camp NothinButNet. We said we'd all keep in touch, and, against the odds, we have. In an amazing show of support, they've come from all across the country to help me launch my professional career.

Twenty minutes until kickoff, and I've got some time to kill. My fan club is sitting on the thirty-five yard line, about twenty rows up. I walk over to their section, and they all come down to the first row to greet me.

Mike has brought a portable TV so they can watch me live from the stands. How cool is that? After all these years of being inseparable, Mike and I have found ourselves half a country apart.

He's at UCLA, where he's majoring in business. We still talk every day and text each other endlessly. Mike was an all-city high school player, but his basketball days were cut short by a knee injury in his senior year. He's on his third girlfriend this semester. I guess some things never change.

Albert Mann grew a lot taller and now has a red goatee to complement his red hair. He drove in from New York, where he's an acting student at NYU. He does stand-up in New York comedy clubs, and I'm sure he'll have his own sitcom someday. He's the funniest guy I know, and still a master of practical jokes.

The guy next to Albert has become a good friend. Rick Craig is 6'4" and is the point guard on Notre Dame's basketball team. Since we're both in Indiana, I go up to South Bend to watch him play and he comes down to Bloomington when I'm announcing games.

After leaving camp that summer, I visited Rick and his family on their ranch in Pennsylvania. Rick taught me how to ride, and I had a great time. He came to visit me the following summer, and we've gotten together every summer since.

A two-year-old boy wearing a Michigan basketball jersey is leaning over the railing. He's got his father's smile and his mother's crystal blue eyes. Tim and Laurie Sanders said they wouldn't miss this for the world. Ever since that first year at camp, we've spoken at least once a month, and they're always available for advice whenever I need it. They really are like part of my family, kind of like an honorary aunt and uncle to me.

"You look great," Lizzie says to me.

"Don't be fooled. It's the four pounds of make-up," Albert cracks.

"I can't tell you how proud we are," Laurie says.

"Now that you're a big-time sportscaster, how are you ever going to have time for little people like us?" Tim asks.

"I'll fit you guys in somehow," I say. "What's your name again?" They all laugh.

Mike takes out a small wrapped gift. "Ernie, my man: as you start your sports broadcasting career, your Camp NothinButNet fan club wants you to have this little 'good luck' gift."

I open the package, look inside, and bust out laughing. It's a banana. Actually, it's one of those refrigerator magnets that look like the real thing.

"I can't believe this. You guys are too much."

"It's to remind you how it all started," Albert says.

"Like I'd ever forget," I say. "Whenever I'm in front of a microphone, I'm going to keep this with me."

Through my earpiece, the producer is telling me to get in place for my first interview. I excuse myself, and they all wish me luck.

The kickoff is two minutes away, but my broadcasting career is starting right now. I'm standing on the sidelines with the Ohio State coach. A camera is on me, and a production assistant counts me down to the live interview. Just before he gives me the "go" signal, I pat the banana inside my left pocket for luck.

"I'm Ernie Dolan with Ohio State coach Marv Sender. Coach, how is your defense going to counter Michigan's massive offensive line, which averages 320 pounds?"

"Ernie, we're going to have to try to beat them with our quickness and hope our linebackers contain any further penetration."

"Thanks, Coach. There it is, folks, a classic battle between strength and speed. This is Ernie Dolan, reporting from the sideline. Back to you, Keith."

Wow! What a rush. Eight million people just saw me on television. Good thing I didn't think of that before the interview. I glance up at my fan club in the stands, all huddled around Mike's TV. They give me a thumbs-up.

I do two more reports in the first half and one in the second. My total air time is two minutes and four seconds, but the memory will last forever.

⊕

After the game, we all get together for dinner. My parents reserved a private room in a nice Italian restaurant. As I walk into the room, the gang starts a quiet indoor chant: "Er-nie! Er-nie! Er-nie!" I thank everyone for coming and making this day so special.

Later that night, when everyone has gone their separate ways, Mike and I are alone as he drives me back to my hotel.

"I'm really proud of you, bud. There's no limit to what you can do. You've gotta work the Super Bowl so you can hook us all up with tickets."

"One job at a time, Mike. But you'll always have tickets waiting for you."

"Hey," Mike says, "did I tell you I'm going to work two weeks at Camp NothinButNet?"

"No. When?"

"Middle of July. I'm going to be a coach and counselor."

"That's great, Mike."

"Here's a thought. If you can, why don't you join me there for a little reunion?"

"I'd love that. I've got to cover some baseball this summer, but if I'm free, I'm there."

"You're really going to come?"

"Why not? It worked out pretty well the first time."

Mike and I share a laugh. I lean back, close my eyes, and think back again to that magical summer and how that camp with the funny name changed my life.

⊕

In spite of everything, I'm still an average guy. There's a lot of us average guys out there, and I'm proud to be one.

The dictionary defines *average* as "being of no special quality or type." Obviously, the people who wrote that dictionary never met any of us.

Acknowledgments

One of the things I've learned from this process is just how hard it is to have a novel published. It takes nothing short of divine intervention, or at the least, the kindness of some very caring strangers.

I'd like to thank Alison Picard for finding a home for this book, as well as my next book. Thank you for your tenacity and not taking "no" for an answer.

My publisher, Evelyn Fazio, got this book from the start. She guided me on a path that made it better with every draft. I am grateful for her attention and contributions, but more so for her belief in me as a writer. Though we have yet to meet, I consider her a friend and enjoy our cross-country conversations.

Writing is a lonely profession and one can only talk to the walls so much. Thankfully, I am blessed with a great family. I want to thank my wife, Susan, and sons, Kevin and Eric, for their never-ending support, patience, and encouragement for this book. If it turns out that they are the only people who read it, this was all worth it.